MW00789926

The Healer

AMISH COUNTRY BRIDES

Jennifer Spredemann

© 2022

Copyright 2022 by Jennifer Spredemann, J.E.B. Spredemann

All rights reserved. No part of this work/book may be copied, transmitted, or stored in any form or by any means, except for brief quotations in printed reviews, without prior written consent from the author/publisher.

All incidents and characters in this book are completely fictional and derived by the author's imagination. Any resemblance to actual incidents and persons living or dead are purely coincidental.

Published in Indiana by *Blessed Publishing*.

www.jenniferspredemann.com

All Scripture quotations are taken from the *King James Version* of the *Holy Bible*.

Cover design by *iCreate Designs* ©

ISBN: 978-1-940492-87-2
10 9 8 7 6 5 4 3 2 1

Get a FREE Amish story as my thank you gift
when you sign up for my newsletter here:
www.jenniferspredemann.com

BOOKS by JENNIFER SPREDEMANN

AMISH BY ACCIDENT TRILOGY
Amish by Accident
*Englisch on Purpose (*Prequel to *Amish by Accident)*
*Christmas in Paradise (*Sequel to *Amish by Accident)* (co-authored with Brandi Gabriel)

AMISH SECRETS SERIES
An Unforgivable Secret - Amish Secrets 1
A Secret Encounter - Amish Secrets 2
A Secret of the Heart - Amish Secrets 3
An Undeniable Secret - Amish Secrets 4
A Secret Sacrifice - Amish Secrets 5 (co-authored with Brandi Gabriel)
A Secret of the Soul - Amish Secrets 6
A Secret Christmas – Amish Secrets 2.5 (co-authored with Brandi Gabriel)

AMISH BIBLE ROMANCES
An Amish Reward (Isaac)
An Amish Deception (Jacob)
An Amish Honor (Joseph)
An Amish Blessing (Ruth)
An Amish Betrayal (David)

COMING 2023 (Lord Willing)
A Forbidden Amish Courtship
A Widower's Amish Courtship

BOOKS by J.E.B. SPREDEMANN
AMISH GIRLS SERIES
Joanna's Struggle
Danika's Journey
Chloe's Revelation
Susanna's Surprise
Annie's Decision
Abigail's Triumph
Brooke's Quest
Leah's Legacy
A Christmas of Mercy – Amish Girls Holiday

Unofficial Glossary
of Pennsylvania Dutch Words

Ach –Oh

Aenti –Aunt

Boppli/Bopplin –Baby/Babies

Bruder/Brieder –Brother/Brothers

Chust –Just

Daed/Dat –Dad

Dawdi –Grandfather

Dawdi haus –A small dwelling typically used for grandparents

Denki –Thanks

Der Herr –The Lord

Dochder(n) –Daughter(s)

Dummkopp –Dummy

Englischer –A non-Amish person

Ferhoodled –Crazy, scatterbrained, mind is elsewhere

Fraa –Wife/Missus

G'may –Members of an Amish fellowship

Gott –God

Gross sohn –Grandson

Gut –Good

Guten tag –Good day, good morning

Herr –Mister/Lord

Jah –Yes

Kapp – Amish head covering

Kinner –Children

Kumm –Come

Maed/Maedel –Girls/Girl

Mamm –Mom

Rumspringa –Running around period for Amish youth

Schatzi –Sweetheart

Schweschder(n) –Sister(s)

Sohn –Son

Wunderbaar – Wonderful

Author's Note

The Amish/Mennonite people and their communities differ one from another. There are, in fact, no two Amish communities exactly alike. It is this premise on which this book is written. I have taken cautious steps to assure the authenticity of Amish practices and customs. Old Order Amish and New Order Amish may be portrayed in this work of fiction and may differ from some communities. Although the book may be set in a certain locality, the practices featured in the book may not necessarily reflect that particular district's beliefs or culture. This book is purely fictional and built around a fictional community, even though you may see similarities to real-life people, practices, and occurrences.

We, as *Englischers*, can learn a lot from the Plain People and their simple way of life. Their hard work, close-knit family life, and concern for others are to be applauded. As the Lord wills, may this special culture continue to be respected and remain so for many centuries to come, and may the light of God's salvation reach their hearts.

ONE

Shiloh Miller was sure of two things.

One, Mikey Eicher was the man she wanted to marry. Two, if her father—Silas—were to ever find out they were still courting, she'd be grounded for the rest of her life.

Which was why she now lay in her bed, as quietly as possible, waiting until she was sure and certain *Mamm* and *Dat* were fast asleep. She clicked on her flashlight and pulled out the letter she'd received from her beloved two days ago. Her eyes roamed the words for the fourth time.

> *Hey, Shi.*
> *I'm getting out of jail on Friday. Will you meet me at your folks' store after they turn in for the night? I'm guessing it'll be about nine or ten. I'll park my car down the road and*

walk to the store and wait until you come out.
I've missed you.
Mikey

Anticipation had kept her stomach in knots all evening. If *Dat* knew she was sneaking out to meet Mikey...

Silas Miller couldn't shake the feeling of uneasiness. He wasn't sure what it was, but it was *something*. Like there was a storm brewing. But storm or not, if he didn't get to sleep soon, he'd be worthless in the metal shop tomorrow. And with the order he and his *bruder* Paul had to fill, they'd both need to be at the top of their game.

He listened intently to the quiet house for a moment. Nothing but the ticktock of the clock in the living room. Everyone appeared to be fast asleep. All was well in the Miller home.

Kayla slept soundly next to him. His hand ached to reach out and touch his *fraa*, but he didn't want to wake her from her slumber. She'd have a busy day too, no doubt.

He sighed, said a silent prayer, then drifted off in peaceful sleep.

Shiloh recalled her last conversation with *Dat* and *Mamm* about her beau. *Dat* had just come home from his men's Bible study at Mikey's *grossdawdi*, Sammy Eicher's, house. Neither *Mamm* nor *Dat* had known she'd still been dating Mikey. *Dat* hadn't been too happy that morning when he discovered that Mikey was in jail, *and* that they had been courting in secret. She knew her folks didn't approve of Mikey or his actions, but they hadn't forbidden their courtship.

Until now.

Dat wanted her to immediately put a stop to their relationship. But she couldn't break up with Mikey—she wouldn't. She loved him. And if she guessed correctly, he needed someone on his side now more than ever. How could she just abandon the love of her life when he needed her most?

She hadn't outright told *Dat* that she would *or wouldn't* break things off with Mikey. But she was positive *Dat* assumed she would obey because he'd told her to. She had never outright defied *Dat*...before tonight.

Her fingers trembled as she imagined what would happen if she and Mikey got caught. *Please don't let us get caught, Gott.*

Shiloh wasn't sure how wise it was to pray to God when she was about to go against her folks' wishes.

But she was twenty-one now. Plenty old enough to make up her own mind about who she wanted to date and marry. If only she were brave enough to utter those words to *Mamm* and *Dat*.

She shined the flashlight on her nightstand clock. *Mamm* and *Dat* had turned in an hour ago. Surely they were asleep by now. She tucked her letter under her pillow and slowly hoisted herself from the bed. Why was it that every little movement she made sounded like it was connected to a speaker, like the ones in Mikey's car?

When she reached the hallway, she stopped to listen. Sure enough, *Dat's* snore escaped through the crack under his and *Mamm's* bedroom door and echoed down the hall. If she could just tiptoe past their room, she could sneak out the front door and no one would be the wiser. Her heart pounded louder than she could think.

The moment she stepped outside, she sighed in relief. *Ach*, the fresh spring air felt so *gut*.

"How's the prettiest girl in the world?" Mikey drew Shiloh into his arms and claimed his first kiss of the evening.

Ach, she'd always loved his kisses. Never could

seem to get enough of being held in Mikey's solid arms.

Mikey's lips strayed from hers. "Mm...Shi...I wanna..."

Shiloh stepped back. "You wanna what?"

He drew her back into his arms and shook his head. "I'm not sure you want to know what I'm thinking, *schatzi*."

"I do. Tell me what's on your mind."

"I want to be with you. I want to live with you. I want to have a *boppli* with you," he murmured as his thumb caressed her cheek.

"Well, we *will* have a *boppli* eventually." She shrugged. "*Gott* willing."

"I mean *now*. Imagine if you were in the *familye* way already," he whispered close to her ear.

She was certain she must've turned watermelon pink at his bold words. She remembered her conversations with her best friend, Lucy, about how that all came about. If her *vatter* were in earshot... "*Ach*, Mikey. You shouldn't say such things. Or want that *yet*. And us not married? *Nee*."

"How do you suppose we would marry in the Amish church when it goes against my church's *Ordnung* and your *vatter* is against us?"

"I don't know." A dilemma, indeed.

"Think about it, *lieb*. It would be a *gut* thing." His

hands were warm as they gently massaged her neck. "Then your folks would insist I marry you. We'd have their blessing."

She gasped. "*Nee. Dat* would be angry."

"*Jah.* He'd get over it quick enough, though."

"I don't want to end up like Lucy."

"Lucy is happily married to Justin Beachy, Shi."

"*Jah*, she's happy *now*. But she didn't marry her *boppli's* father." She pulled back. "And you're still in *rumspringa*."

"She would have married him if he was Amish, though. She knew she wouldn't be happy in the *Englisch* world."

"But you are? Even though you went to jail?"

"That's the thing. I didn't even *have to* go to jail. It was only because of *mei grossdawdi's* insistence. I could have gotten off with just community service had *Grossdawdi* Sammy not put his two cents in. *Dat* always listens to him."

"Don't be mad at your *grossdawdi*."

"I'm beyond mad. I'm furious." His hands clenched at his sides

"Have you been home since you got out?"

His head shook once, and hard. "I'm not going home."

Her breath hitched. "Where will you go, then?"

"The thing is, Shi." He took her hands in his. "I want you to come with me. Please?"

"Go with you? Into the world?" Mikey was planning to leave? She pulled her hands away and tears burned her eyes. "I don't want to be *Englisch*."

"It would only be for a little while, I promise."

"What about Sierra? She'd be lost without me."

"Your *schweschder* will be fine. All your siblings will. And I know your *mamm* will understand, since she was born *Englisch*." He reached over and grasped her hand again. "And I know my *mamm* and *dat* will too. They all spent their time in the *Englisch* world, but they came back."

"*Dat* would never forgive me."

"I know Silas Miller. He's a *very* forgiving man. He might not like me right now, but he'll get over it. Everyone will."

She trembled as she considered his plan. "I'm scared, Mikey."

"You'll be with me, *schatzi*. What's there to be scared of?" He clutched her close and rubbed her back. "You know I would *never* let anything bad happen to you."

His heart beating against her ear helped to soothe her anxiety. There was something about being in

Mikey's arms that lulled her senses. He always had that effect on her.

"Where would we go?" She leaned back and stared into his eyes.

"I have an idea or two about that."

"You do?" She couldn't believe they were actually having this conversation.

"When I was in jail, one of the guys told me about a place. It's a motel, but sometimes they rent rooms out."

"You...you'd want us to live together—to share a room—without being married?" She shook her head. "Mikey, I can't."

"Don't you want to be with me, *schatzi*?" He was doing it again. Those puppy dog eyes that she couldn't resist. Mikey Eicher was surely the handsomest boy she'd ever known. He was quite distracting whenever she attempted to think rationally.

"I do, but...why can't we just get baptized and join the *G'may*?"

"You know why. Detweiler's district doesn't allow courtships with Bontrager's."

"Then move here. That would solve everything, ain't not?"

"You don't understand, Shi. I can't."

"Why?"

"I've been thinking about it. I'm not ready to be Amish for *gut* yet. I have too much *Englisch* in my blood."

"But you said we'd only live away for a little while. Besides, both of your folks were born Amish. If anyone has *Englisch* in their blood, it would be me. My *mamm* was born *Englisch*."

"Which is why you're the perfect one for me, Shi." He brought her hands to his lips.

"I can't do it, Mikey. Please don't ask me to."

"But you've never even tried the *Englisch* world. How do you know you won't like it?"

"That's what I'm afraid of. What if I like it too much, Mikey? I don't want to be apart from my family and friends. Not now, and certainly not forever."

"You're not baptized yet, so it wouldn't be forever. You need to see what it's like outside of your own little world. Otherwise, you'll *always* wonder." He did have a point. "And the *Englisch* world is different than the Amish. There are no rules—no *Ordnung*—that say you have to stay *Englisch* forever. You can choose what you want."

She *had* always wondered about an *Englisch* life. And he was right. The *Englisch* had no *Ordnung* that she'd ever heard of.

9

"Listen, Shi. If we get married in the Amish, it will be the same way. You wouldn't be living with your family anymore and you'd mostly only see your friends at meeting. And they'll be getting married and beginning their own families too. That's just the way life goes."

"But I won't see them at all if we're *Englisch*."

"We can visit." *Ach*, why did he have to make so much sense? "And what about *rumspringa*? Even your *dat* had a *rumspringa*. This would be yours. He won't fault you for it."

All her reasons for resisting were crumbling. "I don't know, Mikey." She nibbled on her *kapp* string.

"I'll tell you what. What if we just *try* it for a little while? If you decide you don't like it, we'll come back."

"We will?"

"But you have to give it a fair chance, okay?"

Her chin trembled. "I've never done anything like this before, Mikey. I don't want to disappoint my folks."

"Do you think they never disappointed their folks? I guarantee you they did. It's just the way of life, Shi. Our parents expect to be disappointed. They don't expect us to perfectly follow every single rule."

"I guess you're right."

"So, are you on board?"

"Only if you have a *gut* plan. I don't want to live in your car."

Mikey laughed. "*Schatzi*, I'd *never* let you live in my car."

TWO

After searching every day for an entire week and finding nothing, Mikey *finally* stumbled upon a place for him and Shiloh to live. It wasn't exactly what he had planned, but he liked this even better than the motel room his friend had suggested, which was currently unavailable. This would be cozier, more private.

Had it just been *dumm* luck or was it a divine nudge that prompted him to glance at the grocery store bulletin board? Just when he'd thought finding a place for him and Shiloh was hopeless, the flier caught his eye. He'd called right away, surprising the landlord, since the man had just posted the rental notice twenty minutes prior.

Mikey made sure to thank *Der Herr* for His providence. As a last-ditch effort, he'd tossed up a prayer asking *Gott* to help him find a place. He hadn't expected *Der Herr* to answer so swiftly and precisely. This rental was close to perfect. It could only be an answer to prayer.

After paying the landlord rent and watching him drive down the long dirt driveway, Mikey now clutched the keys to the travel trailer they'd be occupying. The RV wasn't much, but it sat on the back side of his landlord's two-hundred-acre parcel, so it was somewhat secluded. He had a feeling that living out here would feel very much like camping.

The landlord had even said there was a small pond on the property that they could access. He'd told Mikey he sometimes fished off the small dock or used the pedal boat for leisure. Mikey smiled at the thought of he and Shiloh packing up a picnic lunch and spending a lazy Saturday at the pond.

He laughed. He hardly knew what a lazy Saturday was.

He sunk onto the glider swing that sat outside the trailer and closed his eyes. The only thing he heard was the sound of birds chirping and a gentle breeze blowing through the nearby wooded area.

He couldn't wait to bring Shiloh here. He hoped she wouldn't change her mind about experiencing the *Englisch* world with him. The only thing that would make it even more perfect was if they were husband and wife.

Shiloh had been counting down the days. Mikey had promised to leave a note in her mailbox once he'd secured a place to live. She had been diligent to check the mailbox every day. She'd been waiting over a week now and nervousness began creeping in.

Hopefully, everything was okay with Mikey. She didn't like being away from him this long, even though they'd been apart longer in the past. And then there was his time in jail. Which made her wonder. What would it be like to be in jail? She shivered at the thought of ever having to find out. All she knew was that Mikey hadn't liked it. At all.

If only Mikey could get along with his *grossdawdi* again. *Everybody* loved Sammy—even Mikey before this jail ordeal. She needed to try to convince him to let his anger go. She didn't like seeing him upset. She liked the smiling and happy version of Mikey much better than this grumpy angry one.

Had Mikey even talked to anybody back home since he'd been released? By what he'd said when they'd briefly spoken, she thought not. Did he just plan on leaving without letting his folks know? Surely his *mamm* would worry.

What was Shiloh thinking? Wasn't that what *she* was going to do? Just disappear in the middle of the night? Of course, she'd planned to leave a note so at least her folks would know she was safe with Mikey and hadn't just vanished off the face of the earth.

Shiloh slipped out of the house once again. Since it would be odd for her to be checking the mail at this early morning hour, she made sure to take cat food with her to feed the three felines that claimed this property as their home. Mikey had said he'd drop the letter off overnight, so it was best to check the mailbox before anyone else got to it. She couldn't chance *Mamm* or *Dat* coming to drop off a bill or a letter and finding Mikey's note.

Maybe today would be the day that would change her life. Did she really want change, though? Not really. She was content where she was. But if this had to happen for her to have Mikey in her life, then she would gladly go with him. Because living without him wasn't an option.

They planned to marry—eventually. As soon as Mikey found his way, she was sure and certain he'd make her his bride.

She thought of Lucy now married to Justin Beachy. Her friend's life hadn't turned out how she'd planned, but Shiloh didn't think she'd ever seen Lucy happier. And to think, her best friend actually married a Beachy brother! It was certainly the stuff dreams were made of.

Now, Shiloh only hoped *Der Herr* would make her dreams come true as well. If only Mikey would come back to the Amish and move to Bontrager's district. But then his family would have to shun him, unless Detweiler's district lightened their stance on the two groups intermingling. *Fat chance.*

Why did the leaders have to make things difficult? Wasn't just being Amish *gut* enough? It wasn't like their districts were all *that* different. Having heaters in buggies or not, wearing a certain color shirt or dress, being allowed to drive a tractor—did *any* of those things even matter to *Der Herr*? She certainly didn't think so. It seemed they'd just made up certain rules so they would be different from other districts.

Hadn't the Bible verse that *Dat* read talk about *Gott* looking at the heart? It was man who judged by outside appearances.

Her heart soared the moment she grasped Mikey's letter. He'd found a place and he'd be coming tomorrow night to whisk her off to their new home! *Ach*, she was both thrilled and terrified at the same time.

This new phase in her life would no doubt be an adventure for sure and certain. Whether she was ready or not, life was about to get interesting.

THREE

Shiloh was thankful this was the last time she'd be sneaking out of her folks' home. Her nerves had been on edge all night.

Well in advance of their meetup time, she'd prepared her tote bag full of things Mikey had suggested she bring with her. It had taken some doing—and craftiness—for her to find everything she needed. She had to make sure *Dat* was busy in the shop, *Mamm* and Sierra were working in the store, and the youngest *kinner* were at school or down for their naps before she could sneak into *Mamm* and *Dat's* room to smuggle her personal documents out of the small locked safe they kept under their bed.

She wasn't even sure why she needed all of it, but she couldn't ask Mikey since she had no way to communicate with him. He'd mentioned something about having a cell phone before and she wished she'd thought to ask for the number. Oh well, it wasn't like she'd be needing it now.

Mikey had said he'd meet her in front of her folks' store like they had previously, then they'd walk down the street to where he'd park the car. She'd sensed excitement in his penned words, which seemed to slip right off the page and into her heart. She didn't know if the giddiness she felt was from nerves or anticipation. Perhaps a little of both?

The best thing about all this was that she and Mikey would be together soon. Her heart pounded at the thought of the two of them sharing a place together—their very own place away from their families. It all sounded so romantic.

Mikey had assured her last time they'd spoken that they would have separate sleeping places. She insisted they wouldn't live as a married couple if they weren't married. He'd promised to respect her wishes. Of course, she wasn't so naïve as to think they wouldn't be tempted—especially living on their own. But she'd made up her mind beforehand that she'd save married love for marriage. And that was that.

A few minutes after ten, she left a note on her dresser and slunk out of the quiet house.

Mikey couldn't suppress the thrill that flooded his soul. He and Shiloh were actually going to do this—live out the dream they'd talked about so many times. Of course, their dream hadn't been exactly like this, but it was *gut* enough.

His grin widened the moment she approached. The moonlight reflecting off her teeth told him she was smiling as well. *Gut*. He hoped she'd be excited about this too.

He reached for her hand and pulled her close. "You ready to do this, beautiful?" he whispered.

"Ready as I'll ever be."

He brushed her cheek with a kiss and relieved her of her tote bag. "*Gut*. Let's go."

Hand-in-hand, they hurried down the road, the light of the moon the only thing guiding their way. The closer they came to his waiting vehicle, the quicker his heart beat.

"I'm nervous."

Jah, Mikey could hear it in her voice. He squeezed her hand. "I am too. But it will all work out. You'll see."

"I hope so."

"I can't wait for you to see our place. I think you'll like it."

"The motel room?"

"*Ach*, it's not at the motel. It's even better."

"I can't wait, then." She sighed.

He fished his keys out of his pocket as they approached his car. He reached to open her door.

A bright light suddenly shined in their faces.

"*Ach*!" He thrust his hand in front of his face to block the light. "Who is it?"

"Who do you think?" a voice answered.

"*Dat*?" Shiloh screeched.

The blinding beam finally lowered.

Just when Mikey thought his plan had gone off without a hitch.

"You two have some explaining to do," Silas said. "You'll come back to the house. Right now."

"I'm going with Mikey." Shiloh's small voice quivered.

Ach, he was proud she'd spoken up and asserted her intentions.

"You're twenty-one." Silas said. "You may do as you choose. But not without telling your mother and *schweschder* goodbye."

Mikey sighed in relief. Silas wasn't going to stop them?

"Let's drive back?" Silas eyed Mikey.

"*Jah*. Sure." Mikey opened the door and rolled the seat forward so Shiloh could sit in the back. Silas took the passenger's side. Mikey slid in and started the car.

"This doesn't mean I'm condoning your actions.

But if you two have your minds made up on going your own way, I at least want to know where my *dochder* is going to be and how she can be contacted. Her mother and I deserve at least that courtesy, don't you think?"

"*Jah*, for sure." Mikey swallowed hard as he drove the short distance and turned into the Millers' lane. Time to face the music.

FOUR

Shiloh's hands trembled as she and Mikey sat at her folks' dinner table waiting for *Dat* to bring out *Mamm* and Sierra. Her hands refused to stop—even when Mikey reached over and placed his hand over hers.

"It'll be okay," he whispered. Easy for him to say when it wasn't his folks they were facing. If only Mikey's words were true.

She couldn't speak for fear of tears falling.

"Shi, you're still coming with me, ain't not?" She heard the uncertainty in his voice.

She shrugged, not trusting her words.

Just then, she heard footsteps entering the living room from the hallway. She didn't dare look up.

"Shiloh and Mikey have something to tell everyone." *Dat's* words were matter-of-fact and void of emotion.

She lifted her eyes to Mikey, but saw *Mamm*, Sierra, *Dat*, and Judah in her peripheral view.

Mikey cleared his throat and Shiloh watched him as he looked at each one standing around the table. She wished they'd all sit down.

"I...uh...Shiloh and I are moving to our own place," Mikey said.

"Your own place?" *Mamm* looked confused. "What do you mean?"

Mikey attempted to prompt Shiloh to speak by nudging her hand, but she didn't want to.

"Shiloh, no." Sierra's voice wavered, and her hand squeezed Shiloh's shoulder. "You're going into the world? And you and Mikey are going to *live* together?" Her voice screeched. She plopped down into the chair next to Shiloh.

Shiloh's eyes lifted to her *schweschder's*, conveying an apology.

"I'm not ready for you to leave me," Sierra continued. "And what about the store? And the *kinner*? Me and *Mamm* can't do it all."

Shiloh finally spoke. "It would be the same if we were getting married."

"No, it wouldn't. If you were married, you'd still be Amish and you could still work in the store," Sierra reasoned. "You won't be allowed to if you're *Englisch*."

"Not if we got married in Detweiler's district," Shiloh said.

"Detweiler's won't allow you to marry Mikey. You know that." *Dat* reminded her.

"Why don't you marry here, then?" *Mamm* seemed to have found her voice again.

"Mikey's not ready to get married yet," Shiloh glanced at *Mamm* and *Dat*.

Mamm's gaze flew to Mikey. "But you want her to *move in* with you?" Her voice tweaked up a notch.

Red stain crept up Mikey's neck and face.

"You and *Dat* and Mikey's folks all had a chance to live *Englisch* for a while. We want the same chance," Shiloh challenged.

"I was born an *Englischer*. And *Dat* only went on a trip during his *rumspringa*. He never ventured out to live in the *Englisch* world," *Mamm* said.

"We're not allowed to even fellowship or date in my folks' Amish district, though." Mikey interjected. "Those rules don't exist among the *Englisch*. We can do what we want if we're *Englisch*."

Dat cleared his throat. "Dating rules, maybe. But you *will not* live together as husband and wife, not being married. *Gott's* laws are higher than Amish or *Englisch* rules." *Dat's* arms crossed over his chest. "Do I make myself clear?"

Mikey glanced at Shiloh, then at *Dat*. "*Jah*."

"Anyway, I thought the least they could do was come in and say goodbye," *Dat* said. "Mikey, if you have a cell phone number, I'd like you to write it down. And the address where you'll be living with my *dochder*."

Mikey grimaced. "I don't have the address memorized yet, but I can call and leave a message."

Dat gave a curt nod. "Tomorrow."

Mikey's gaze slid back to Shiloh. "Remind me, okay?"

Shiloh nodded, then stood from the table. She proceeded to hug each of her family members present. She'd been surprised that Judah, who stood stiff as a board, hadn't uttered a word. Her older *bruder* always had something to say. But apparently not tonight.

"Does Lucy know yet?" Sierra studied her.

"*Nee*. I haven't told her," Shiloh said. "No one knows but you."

"Bailey's gonna flip. Don't be surprised if the lot of us show up on your doorstep," Sierra warned.

Shiloh tittered. "Okay."

Mikey grasped Shiloh's hand in his, and they made their way to the door.

"Isn't anybody going to stop them?" Judah finally spoke up.

When Shiloh turned around, she noticed Judah's scowl.

"They're both adults. If this is the way they choose to live their lives, there's nothing we can do to stop them." *Dat* squeezed Judah's shoulder. "They both know wrong from right. I trust they will make *gut* and wise decisions."

"And the two of them living together is a *gut* and wise decision?" Judah protested. "Seems to me they're opening the door wide for sin."

"Judah," *Mamm* said, "they have a right to make their own choices, whether they be *gut* or bad."

Judah glared at *Mamm*, his stare accusing. "*Jah*, like you did with Josiah Beachy, right?"

"That's enough, *sohn*." *Dat* reprimanded. "We don't need to bring up past mistakes *Der Herr* has already forgiven."

"What I don't understand is why nobody is stopping them. Everyone is just acting like this is okay, and it isn't. They're going off to live in sin and pleasure. They're forsaking the Amish ways. They're not following *Der Herr*." Judah spoke with so much conviction.

"Judah." Shiloh frowned. "I appreciate your concern. But Mikey and I won't be sharing a bed. We spoke about that before I agreed to this. If you think we'll be tempted to, then pray for us. Okay?"

"I still don't like it." Judah grimaced. "I don't trust a man who just got out of jail. Not with my *schweschder*."

Honestly, she was touched by her *bruder's* heartfelt protest. "I love you, Judah." She looked at *Mamm*, *Dat*, and Sierra. "All of you."

Mikey's hands grasped the steering wheel as he maneuvered the car out of the Millers' driveway. He glanced at Shiloh. "Wow, that was…"

"Hard." Shiloh finished Mikey's sentence.

"But they let us go."

"Like *Mamm* and *Dat* said, they had no choice." Shiloh frowned. "I'm sorry that Judah brought up you being in jail. I wish he wouldn't have."

"Well, it is a fact." He shrugged. "You don't regret coming with me already, do you?"

"I'm with the person I love more than anything. How could I?"

He reached over and grasped her hand. "I'd hoped you would see it that way. I love you, Shi."

Her beautiful grin lit up the interior of his vehicle. "I love you too, Mikey."

FIVE

"Where are we going?" Shiloh's hands twisted in her lap as she attempted to see the scenery in the darkness.

"You'll see. It's in the country. Not too far." Mikey glanced her way and grinned. "It's only about ten minutes from your folks' place by car."

"I'm glad it's not really far away."

Mikey turned onto what appeared to be a dirt road.

"Are we here?" Her heart rate sped up. *Ach*, this was exciting.

"I wish we had more light so you could see."

The cars' headlights shown on a small travel trailer. An outdoor light illuminated the entrance, but she only saw a door and metal steps.

"What do you think? Wait until you see the inside." He parked the car to the side of the trailer, then came around and opened the door for her. "Let's go see it."

He slid his hand in hers and slung her bag over his other arm. "There's a couple of steps, so beware when you come back out. I almost missed one and would've ended up face-first in the grass if I hadn't caught myself." He chuckled.

Enthusiasm oozed off him and Shiloh couldn't help being affected by it.

He unlocked the door, held it open, then gestured for her to enter. His hand slipped just inside the door, and he flipped on a light switch. "Let's hurry so we don't let bugs inside."

Shiloh stepped into the travel trailer, and he quickly followed her up the steps and shut the door.

She looked around taking it all in, her mouth opening slightly. "*Ach*, it's so cute. It's like a little bitty house."

"Right? Look, this couch can be turned into a bed. As can the table where we'll take our meals. Then there's sleeping quarters in the back and a larger bed in front—it's like a little bedroom. I figured you could sleep there." He walked to the front and slid open a door. "See? There's a closet for your things and some drawers. And you even have a TV."

"I love it, Mikey!"

"It's just like camping, ain't so? Except that this is much better than the tent we always used." He entwined his fingers with hers and pulled her close, claiming a quick kiss. "What do you think? Do you like it, for real?"

"I do." She smiled and kissed him again.

"I need to show you the bathroom. You can just use it like normal, but don't let the water run longer than necessary. We'll have to refill the tank once in a while. Oh, and there's even a tiny shower."

Her cheeks heated. *Ach*, she hadn't thought about all that. It would be awkward taking a shower with Mikey right on the other side of the door. And judging by the size of the bathroom, it was too small to get dressed in there.

"Anyhow, it's getting late. We should probably turn in for the night. I expected to get back sooner, but..." He shrugged. "We can check out the place more thoroughly tomorrow when the sun is up."

"Is there food here?"

"Not much. I thought we could figure out what all we need, then take a trip into town tomorrow." He opened a cabinet in the kitchen area. "They do keep some cooking supplies in here and said we could use them. I bought some eggs, so we can fry some of those up for breakfast."

"Mikey," Shiloh couldn't help her tears of joy. "This is going to be so *wunderbaar*."

"I feel the same way. And I get to share it with the girl of my dreams." He pulled her into his arms again and gently kissed her lips. "Goodnight, my Shi love."

Silas knew he wouldn't get any work done today without a trip to the Eichers' place. He highly doubted Michael and Sammy knew what Mikey was up to.

With everything in him, he'd wanted to command Mikey to go back home last night and stay away from his *dochder*, but he realized that would likely cause them to rebel even more. He hated the thought of his innocent girl being swayed by Mikey Eicher's charms. If the *bu* was anything like his father...

Silas allowed his mind to wander to his first *fraa*, Sadie Ann. Shortly after they'd married, she'd confessed to briefly dating Michael Eicher. Silas admitted to having some very unchristian thoughts toward his now-friend when he'd learned Sadie Ann had given herself away to him.

Silas hadn't known his first wife then, being a newcomer to the area. But he knew Mike from the time they'd both lived in Pennsylvania. Michael hadn't gotten along well with his folks, which was why he ended up with his *dawdi* Sammy.

Praise God for Sammy Eicher. He'd done what had seemed impossible—brought Mike back from his worldly ways. Of course, Sammy would never take the credit. *Nee*, he gave glory to *Gott* for all of it. But Silas knew that if Sammy hadn't been willing to take Michael in and share *Der Herr's* love, his friend would probably still be out barhopping and chasing women. Silas had never seen someone changed so dramatically. Thankfully, Mike was a completely different man now, in that respect.

Like a *gut* Amish man should, Silas had forgiven both Michael Eicher and Sadie Ann. But forgiveness didn't mean one should just throw caution to the wind. *Nee*, because every man was subject to fall.

Of course, Silas would never claim to be a perfect Christian. He had issues of his own, pride being one of them. And hadn't it been the sin of pride that caused Lucifer's fall in the garden?

He sighed as he maneuvered his horse into the Eichers' driveway. Normally, he'd hire a driver to go this distance, but he'd needed some time alone to clear his thoughts and appeal to *Der Herr* on his *dochder's* behalf. That, and he pleaded for wisdom regarding this situation.

Michael Eicher's ears perked up as a buggy approached and turned into their lane.

Silas Miller?

Not that seeing Silas was odd. *Nee*, they saw each other every week at their men's Bible study group—something the leaders had reprimanded his *dawdi* about on more than one occasion. But seeing Silas on a weekday and driving his buggy *was* an odd occurrence.

Michael strode toward the hitching post as Silas tethered his mare. "Silas, what brings you way out here? Something on your mind?"

"Hey, Mike." His friend half-smiled and nodded. "Is Sammy around?"

"*Jah*. He's just checking out my work in the field." Michael chuckled. "Making sure I planted everything just so."

Silas laughed. "Doesn't trust you, huh?"

"Between you and me, I think he's just antsy for something to do. He took a couple of the *kinner* out with him. Probably teaching them all about the Garden of Eden and the fall of man and all that."

"He never misses an opportunity, does he?" Silas glanced toward the field, a look of admiration in his eye.

"Not that I can tell. But he'd argue that point."

Michael grinned. "I think Miri's got some sweet tea in the house. Would you like a glass?"

"That'd be great."

SIX

"Did I hear we had company?" *Dawdi's* voice hollered from behind the screen door.

"*Jah*, it's Silas Miller," Michael called back from the dining room table. He smiled at Miri. "Would you mind keeping the *kinner* occupied for a little bit, *schatzi*? We've got some business to take care of."

She hefted a basket of laundry. "I've got this laundry to put up, so they'll be out for a while."

Michael relieved his *fraa* of the heavy basket and followed her toward the door. "Second load?"

"Third. I'm thankful to have so many helpers." She reached for the hand of their second youngest. "Keep an ear out for Gracie, would you? She'll be waking up before too long and wanting to eat."

"Of course." He gestured toward Silas as they passed *Dawdi*. "Silas is at the table. I think he wants to speak with both of us. I'll be back in after I carry this out for Miri."

After seeing his wife off with a quick kiss, he hurried back inside. "What's on your mind, Silas?"

Dawdi had already helped himself to a glass of tea and was seated at the head of the table.

"It's *mei dochder*. And your *sohn*." Silas frowned.

"Oh, no." Michael rolled his eyes. "What did he do?"

"He convinced Shiloh to jump the fence with him." He grimaced. "They tried to sneak away last night under the cover of darkness, but I hauled them back in so Shiloh could give her *mamm* and *schweschder* a proper goodbye."

"*Ach*, I'm sorry, man." Unfortunately, Mikey carried many of his father's traits. Fortunately, he wasn't near as bad as *he* had been as a younger man. But somehow, he didn't think sharing that bit of information would be comforting to Silas. "He hasn't been back home since going to jail. He made it clear that he was upset about the whole thing."

"He's mostly upset with me," *Dawdi* interjected.

Silas's forehead wrinkled. "Why would he be upset with you?"

"He could have gotten off with just community service. But I'm not sure that would have taught him a lesson. It starts with something small, like engraving your initials into a covered bridge—"

Silas's eyebrows lifted. "Is that what he did?"

"I know that vandalism or *criminal mischief*, as they called it, doesn't sound like much. But if Mikey thinks he can get away with it, that might lead to something more daring or dangerous. I didn't want him to go down that road." *Dawdi* shrugged. "I figured that if he went to jail, that would be enough deterrent to where he wouldn't want to go back."

"Do you think it worked?"

"It must have. I think that's why he's so angry about it. Jail is no picnic. And I imagine it's quite a bit worse than in my day." *Dawdi* grimaced.

"Wait." Silas's eyes widened. "Are you saying *you've* been in jail, Sammy?"

Michael chuckled. "I know. I couldn't believe it either."

"More than once." *Dawdi* lifted his palms. "What? You think all these gray hairs are here because of old age? Or Michael?"

"Hey!" Michael chuckled. "Okay, *jah*. Probably *some* of them are from me." He admitted. Probably most of them, now that he thought about it.

Dawdi sniggered.

Silas scrubbed his beard. "I can't imagine *you* being in jail."

41

"We're all sinners, *sohn*." *Dawdi* eyed both of them, more sober now. "I was even more thickheaded than Mikey. That's why I believe he needed to see how difficult life can be. That *bu* is a smart fellow."

"But he's living with *mei dochder*." Silas frowned. "Somehow, I don't see this ending well for her."

"And if it doesn't, she'll *still* learn the lesson *Der Herr* has for her. You *chust* need to show her grace and let her know that you are there for her—even *if* she falls. That is what a *gut vatter* does." *Dawdi* nodded. "I think it takes great wisdom to know when to leave the ninety-nine to fetch the lost one and when to patiently wait for the prodigal to return."

Michael's heart clenched thinking about all his own failures. "That's what you had to do with me, ain't not?"

"*Jah*. And you about wore my patience thin." *Dawdi's* wry chuckle made Michael think that remark hadn't been far from the truth.

"Times like this might be hard, but they are *gut* for us. They make us realize our need for *Der Herr*. If we never had trials, we'd have no need to call on *Gott* for help." *Dawdi* sipped his tea. "Not only that, but they also strengthen our faith."

Dawdi bowed his head. "Let's pray, shall we?"

SEVEN

A slight rocking motion propelled Shiloh to sit up on the bed, her eyelids protesting the brightness coming through the windows. Yummy scents tickled her nose. Was it bacon? *Ach,* she was late helping *Mamm* and Sierra get breakfast on the table. Except...she finally opened her eyes and realized where she was.

"Oh good, you're awake." Mikey's head poked around the sliding door of the trailer's small bedroom. "I made us some breakfast. Are you hungry?"

Her eyes widened. "*You* made breakfast?"

"Sure did."

She caught the pride in his voice, then she groaned. "Why didn't you wake me up? I could have made it."

"I wanted to let my princess sleep. And I was hoping it would be a pleasant surprise."

"*Ach,* you're adorable." She glanced down at her

nightgown. "Uh, I'll be out in just a couple of minutes, okay?"

Instead of leaving, he stood there grinning like a fool.

"What? If you think you're going to watch me change, you've got another thing coming. Boyfriends don't get husband privileges." She shook a teasing finger at him.

"Hey." He lifted both hands. "You can have your privacy. I'm just happy to see your beautiful face first thing in the morning, that's all. I'll get out of your hair now."

Shiloh smiled to herself as Mikey slid the door closed again. All of a sudden, she felt giddy. Not only were they living here on their own, but Mikey made her breakfast!

It pleased Mikey to do something special for Shiloh. He realized that he actually *liked* cooking. There was something satisfying about beginning with raw ingredients and creating something that tasted amazing. And he *knew* it was amazing because he'd sampled the food. It wouldn't have been very fun to set something inedible down in front of his sweetheart.

She finally emerged from her cave, looking gorgeous as ever. She'd worn one of his favorite colors today.

"Mm...you have to be the most beautiful girl in the world." He loved seeing her eyes light up at his words. "Come, sit."

She did as suggested, and Mikey sat on the opposite side of the small table. He slid a cup of orange juice toward her.

Her smile didn't leave her face. "I thought you said there weren't any groceries. How did you come up with all this?"

"I said we didn't have *many* groceries. And *this*?" He gestured to their meal. "I had all planned out."

"You know you're spoiling me, right?"

He reached over and grasped her hand. "I hope so."

"Should we pray?" She lifted her eyebrow.

"Right." He bowed his head and spoke a few silent words of thanks. He cleared his throat. "What do you want first?"

"How about some of that bacon?"

"*Gut* choice. Do you want some of everything?" He scooped up eggs with a spatula.

"Sure. But not too much. I don't eat near as much as you do." She took a bite of the eggs. "These are yummy. You did a *gut* job."

"Do you mean it? You really like it?" He craved her praise.

She bit into the bacon and nodded.

"I'm glad." He gestured toward the window. "After breakfast, I'd like to show you around. Then we can go into town and do some shopping."

"That sounds *gut*."

"Oh, I called your folks' phone shanty and left the address with them. Hopefully, that will put their minds at ease."

"*Gut*." She sipped her orange juice, eyeing him in admiration.

Ach, he didn't think he could ever get enough of that look in her eye.

Shiloh squinted in the bright sunshine.

"Well, now that we've got light, what do you think?"

"I think I might need to buy a pair of sunglasses," she teased.

"Look, we have a swing so we can sit out here and watch the sunset. And if we wanted to stay outside longer, we could use the firepit. I was thinking we could pick up some marshmallows to roast when we go to the store."

he loved the enthusiasm in Mikey's voice. She'd never seen him this happy before.

"S'mores?"

"If you'd like." His excitement was contagious.

"You're right. It does feel like camping."

"Come on." He reached for her hand. "Let's take a walk. I want to show you something else."

"There's more?" Her eyes widened.

"You'll see."

They walked hand in hand along a path through a wooded area. When they came out on the other side, her breath was stolen away. An expansive pond glistened in the morning sun, begging her to dip her toe in.

"Isn't it nice?"

"*Ach*, Mikey! It's *wunderbaar*. Can we swim in it?"

He nodded several times. "And fish. And we can even use the little pedal boat if we want."

She walked out onto the small dock, taking in the beauty around them. "Do you know how deep it is?"

"No." He gestured to a shaded area. "I thought we could bring a picnic lunch out here once in a while. What do you think?"

"I think that sounds perfect. I could bring a book and just sit out here and read." She released a wistful sigh.

He snatched her hand again and coaxed her into his arms. He leaned down and claimed a kiss. "I think you're perfect."

"We make a *gut* team, I think."

He nuzzled her ear. "You know what I think?"

Ach. It was hard to concentrate when he did romantic stuff like that. "What?"

His lips met hers again, lingering even longer than the last kiss. He drew her closer, tilted his head, and slowly deepened the kiss. One of his hands tenderly massaged her neck, and the other held her at the waist. Mikey had to be the sweetest, gentlest kisser ever.

He finally pulled back. "I think you need to marry me."

EIGHT

Shiloh blinked, her eyes searching his. "Marry you?"

"Mm-hm." He tucked a strand of hair behind her ear. "What do you think?"

"You mean, go back and join the church?"

He shook his head. "No. No church. Just you and me, an *Englisch* preacher, and *Gott*. At the courthouse."

She frowned. Not the reaction he'd been hoping for. "But I want an Amish wedding. *Mamm* and *Dat* and Sierra and my aunts and uncles and everyone will want to be there to share our special day. And what about the *Eck*? I already have plans for it. I have my special dishes in my hope chest."

Ach. Of course. He hadn't thought about all that. "Well, what if we...?" He shook his head. "Nah."

"What if we *what*?"

"I was just thinking. What if we got married in the

Englisch world anyway? We don't have to tell anyone back home that we got hitched. It can be our secret."

Shiloh's lips pressed together, and her brow lowered.

"You could still have an Amish wedding later." He shrugged. "Besides, I kind of told the landlord that we were."

Her eyes flew wide. "Were what?"

"Already married." He grimaced. "I didn't want him to say no to us getting the trailer."

Her hand settled on the curve of her hip. "Mikey. That's not right."

"I know. But I hoped that you'd say yes. And if you do, it won't be a lie anymore."

"I don't know, Mikey." She pulled one of her perfectly kissable lips between her teeth, which told him she was at least pondering the idea. *Gut*.

"Think about it, Shi. If we do marry, living here together won't be so *verboten*."

"But what if somebody finds out? Then we wouldn't get to marry Amish."

"Nobody will find out unless we tell them." He reached for her hand, his eyes pleading. His fingers brushed her cheek. "I'd like more than anything to have you as my *fraa*. I love you, Shiloh."

"Mikey...I'm just, I'm nervous." Indecision warred

in the depths of her eyes. "I do want to, but how long do you think we'll be *Englisch*?"

"I'll tell you what. Let's make a deal." He grinned. "You marry me now, and we'll go back to your folks' district, go through baptism classes, and marry *this* fall. If you still have your heart set on that. What do you say?"

"This fall?" She nibbled her lip again.

"Mm-hm."

Shiloh's hands trembled as she and Mikey stood in front of the justice of the peace. She still couldn't believe they were doing this, but here they were. She closed her eyes, praying they were doing the right thing.

Ach, this was so different than a many-hours-long Amish wedding day filled with family, friends, food, and fun activities.

Nobody from their communities were there except the two of them. They even had strangers present as their two witnesses.

Even her best friend Lucy, who'd been in the family way, had an Amish wedding.

But then, Mikey promised they'd still get baptized and have their Amish wedding. She'd still have her special day with family, friends, food, and fun fellowship among their loved ones. Everything would be okay. It would all work out.

Mikey took her hands in his and repeated the words the officiant said with conviction in his voice and sincerity in his gaze. Shiloh did the same thing. She'd meant the words with all her heart, and she was certain Mikey did too. *Ach*, she loved this man so much!

When the justice of the peace pronounced them husband and wife, Mikey leaned forward and kissed her lips. And although there were only a few other people present, her cheeks still felt hot over his public display of affection.

After signing the final documents, they walked out of the courthouse. She was now Mrs. Michael Eicher Jr.!

"Let's do something special, *jah*?" He opened the car door for her.

"Like what?"

"I don't know. Do you want to go somewhere?"

"Like, out to lunch? Or do you mean on a honeymoon?" Her pulse sped up at the thought.

"Both." His grin widened. "Just for a few days, maybe. I'll need to get back to work at the feedstore next week. I took a little time off."

"That sounds like fun. Where should we go?"

"You decide." He turned in the seat, his eyes gleaming with love. *Ach*, she couldn't believe they were husband and wife!

"Well, I was thinking maybe the Smokey Mountains like Justin and Lucy, but how about...?" Excitement filled her.

"How about...?" His eyebrow hitched upward.

"Would you want to go see the ocean? I've never been, have you?"

"*Nee.*" His face could hardly contain his smile, it seemed. He looked so happy, and Shiloh's heart couldn't help but agree. "Let's do it."

"For real?" She squealed.

"For real. Let's go. Right now." He leaned over and kissed her lips, then the engine roared to life.

NINE

Silas walked backed to the house with Shiloh's new address in hand. He was grateful Mikey had made *gut* on his word about letting him know where they'd be living, although he wasn't sure exactly where the place was. He'd need to ask one of the drivers to use their GPS to locate the property.

Mikey had said the dwelling he was renting was a trailer. Why Shiloh would choose to live in a trailer rather than a perfectly *gut* Amish home was beyond him. But then, when he and Kayla were dating, he'd been crazy about her and probably would have lived anywhere to be with her. Still would, in fact. He needed to remind himself what young love was like and all the emotions that went with it.

It was those very emotions he was worried about. Would Mikey convince Shiloh to do things they shouldn't? He promised he'd respect her. But then again, he'd also already talked her into rebelling against her folks' wishes and moving in within him.

Perhaps Silas should make it a point to visit now and then to make sure Mikey was keeping his word. Everyone could use a little accountability. And since Shiloh was still his *dochder* and unmarried, he had an obligation to her and *Der Herr* to make sure that she was protected and provided for.

Jah, it would be *gut* to see where his *dochder* would be living. He needed to talk to Kayla to see if they could get away tomorrow evening after the store closed for the day.

Mikey yawned and glanced over at the passenger seat where his *fraa* had nodded off. *His fraa!* He could hardly believe they were married. He'd dreamt about having her as his wife since Justin Beachy's wedding. He'd forever be grateful he'd been asked to be one of the *newhockers* with Shiloh as his partner. And then when he discovered it had been Shiloh who'd made the suggestion, his heart had soared.

He'd had a crush on her ever since their families had a frolic at his folks' place. He'd only been fourteen then and Shiloh eleven, but she'd caught his eye just the same. He'd only seen her occasionally after that, because they lived in different districts, but he remembered her well. Then after the wedding three years ago, they communicated off and on then eventually started dating. And now, ten years after they met, they were hitched at last.

He pulled into the motel parking lot, then leaned over and kissed her soft cheek.

Her eyes fluttered open.

"It's too far to drive the entire way tonight. We can sleep here then be on our way in the morning." He unbuckled her seatbelt. "Sound *gut*?"

She yawned. "*Jah*. How long have I been asleep?"

"An hour or so. I can't imagine sleeping upright can be very comfortable."

She tilted her neck from side to side. "You're right. A bed sounds *wunderbaar*."

"Especially with my *fraa* next to me."

Her cheeks darkened at his comment, and she dipped her head.

Shiloh stared up at the motel sign. She wanted to remember the place where she and Mikey would be celebrating their first night as husband and wife.

"Here, let's take a selfie with the motel in the background!" Mikey held up his cell phone. "Later, we can have our photos printed and put them in an album. I'm glad we have a couple from the courthouse. This day should be preserved."

"We can take some at the beach too." She beamed. *Ach*, being with Mikey was the best thing ever.

"That sounds perfect." He stood next to her, slipped his arm around her back, and snapped a couple shots. His grin widened. "Are you ready?" He raised a brow.

She got the feeling he was talking about more than just going inside the building. Was she ready to begin life as his *fraa*? Anticipation warmed her from the inside out. "*Jah*. I'm ready."

Hand in hand, they walked into their future—one where they'd always be together.

TEN

If Mikey lived a thousand years, he didn't think he'd ever get enough of Shiloh Eicher. *Ach*, life with her had been amazing so far. She was the epitome of everything wonderful. Sunshine, air, water, joy—his very breath, it seemed. How had he lived this long without her?

He'd made a terrible mistake, though.

How could he keep his promise to her of an Amish wedding *now*? There was no way he'd be able to stay away from his beloved *fraa* for months, which was exactly what he would have to do if they went back to the Amish. How on earth could they pretend they weren't married now that they were, as the Bible succinctly put it, one flesh? How could they pretend to be normal?

He hadn't realized marriage would have this effect on him. He dreaded the thought of even going back to work because he'd have to be apart from her many hours during the day. He didn't want to be without her for one minute. He didn't just *want* her. He needed her as much as he needed the air in his lungs.

"What's wrong? Why are you frowning?" Shiloh's hand rubbed his forearm.

He changed lanes, then glanced her way. "I was just thinking. I don't know how we're going to live apart when we go back to the Amish."

"I actually had an idea about that." She tugged her bottom lip between her teeth, distracting him from the road.

If he had his way, he'd pull over on the side of the road right now and kiss her senseless.

"What?" Her smile brightened up the car.

"I'm crazy in love with *mei fraa*, that's what." He captured her hand and kissed it.

She giggled. "You're cute."

"What was your idea?"

"I was thinking that since you're going to move to Bontrager's district, maybe you could stay in the *dawdi haus*."

"Do you think your folks would let me?" Excitement thumped in his chest. Next door to Shiloh? *Jah*, he could do next door.

"I don't see why not. In their eyes, it would be a

step forward for us. I mean, we're already living together. There, we'd be close but living apart." She shrugged. "Maybe that could be a condition of us coming back. And you could offer to pay rent."

"That's right. That's the perfect solution, I think." His hand grazed her cheek. "You're so *schmart*."

"Do you think we could stop and visit *Mamm* and *Dat* when we get back? I was thinking that I'm going to have quite a few hours by myself during the day once you go back to work. I would like to pick up my soapmaking supplies from the house. That would keep me busy when I run out of things to do in our tiny trailer."

"You could always watch TV all day." He teased.

"Michael Eicher Junior! Bite your tongue. You know I could never sit around staring at a box all day."

"It would be an interesting box." He raised a brow.

"*Nee*. Not to me. I'd go mad."

He grinned. "I do like your soaps."

"They smell *gut*, *ain't not*? I love when you use that woodsy one I gave you. It just makes me want to kiss you."

"Oh, it does, huh?" He chuckled. "I'll have to remember that."

His cell phone vibrated on the console between them, and he glanced down at it.

"What was that?"

"It looks like a call from your folks' phone shanty. Remind me to call back when I'm not driving."

Since Silas hadn't been able to get ahold of Mikey Eicher, he probably shouldn't have spent money to hire a driver to take him and Kayla to see Shiloh. But that fact made the short trip seem even more urgent.

He glanced out the vehicle's window at the property where Shiloh was reportedly living. A long driveway took them down a grassy path that led to a small camping trailer. A wooded area gave privacy on every side. The property and trailer were actually quite a bit nicer than what Silas had imagined.

"Is this the place? I don't see any cars." Kayla peeped over the back of her seat at him. Since they'd hired a female driver, Silas had opted for the backseat.

"I think so. We'll knock anyway." He stepped out and turned to their driver. "Would you mind staying just a bit? I'm not sure anyone is home."

He and his *fraa* strode up the small walkway to the trailer. A somewhat new glider swing sat under the trailer's awning and a small firepit with upturned logs encircling it reminded Silas of a few of the get-togethers the young folks had when he and his first *fraa* were courting.

Since he'd been a widower when he and Kayla met, they'd missed out on all the youth activities that usually accompanied courting. The thought that Kayla missed out on so much saddened him a bit. But he reckoned she missed out on much more than that, being in the *familye* way at sixteen.

"It looks decent, doesn't it?" Silas arched a brow.

"*Jah*. It's cozy. It reminds me of growing up and camping with my parents. We always went at least a few times a year."

Maybe she hadn't missed out on too much. It was a shame he'd never had a chance to meet her folks. They seemed like *gut* people who cared much for their *dochder*.

"It looks like they could have their own campground out here." Silas turned a circle, viewing the meadow that butted up to the tree line. "Plenty of room for tents."

"Are you suggesting we come here and camp out?" Kayla laughed. "I'm sure that would put a damper on any of Mikey's romantic notions."

"If he has romantic notions in mind, I doubt that would dampen them much. Do you remember what it was like being their age?" He winked.

"Of course. How can I forget? We had a romantic notion or two of our own." Her eyes sparkled with mischief.

"Think we should leave a note to let them know we stopped by?"

"Sure. I have some paper and a pen in my purse." She dug into her brown leather bag and handed them to Silas.

He jotted a quick note with a request for Shiloh to call, then the two of them headed back home.

Somehow, Silas felt a little bit of relief now that he'd seen their place. It seemed like a *gut* option for a young married couple. Except, Shiloh and Mikey *weren't* married. Which caused worry to creep back in.

Where were they?

ELEVEN

Phone in hand, Mikey stepped out onto the balcony of their high-rise hotel room sporting brand new swim trunks. Shiloh whistled playfully and he leaned down to kiss his gorgeous *fraa*, who sunbathed on the porch in the modest swimsuit he'd purchased for her. Well, it was the most modest one he could find at the souvenir shop outside their hotel, anyhow.

She hadn't been totally uncomfortable with the idea since the *youngie* in their district sometimes gathered at a local swimming spot. Mikey had been somewhat surprised when she'd mentioned it. Not surprised that they had a place for the *youngie* to gather, but that her folks had allowed her and her siblings to go. He'd always seen Silas as the conservative type, although Bontrager's district was less strict than Detweiler's, where Mikey was from.

It seemed like many of the Amish he knew allowed their teenagers to be normal teenagers. Apparently, her folks must've taken that approach too. Perhaps his dating Shiloh had been a little more than they'd been willing to tolerate.

Of course, they'd been fine with it up until he'd gone to jail. He scowled, thinking of his brief stint there, which had been totally avoidable and unnecessary. *Dat* had been ready to post bail when *Grossdawdi* butted in and offered his two cents.

He scowled, then remembered the task at hand. He needed to get this phone call to Shiloh's father over with so he and his *fraa* could enjoy their secret honeymoon in peace.

"Hey, Silas, this is Mikey. Sorry we missed you. Shiloh and I are out of town for a few days, but we should be back by Tuesday. You can call me back if you want." A moment after Mikey tapped the End button, his phone vibrated. He glanced at Shiloh. "*Ach*, it looks like your *dat* calling back."

"Hello?" He called into the phone.

"It's Silas. Where are you two? Kayla and I stopped by your place."

"You did?" His eyes widened. "*Jah*, well, we decided to take a trip to the coast. We're in Virginia." He briefly thought of the sign they'd seen driving in boasting, *Virginia is for lovers*. He hoped her *vatter* wasn't thinking about that at this moment.

"You drove all the way to Virginia with my *dochder*?" *Ach*, irritation spiked Silas's voice. *Jah*, he was upset.

Mikey rubbed the back of his neck. "*Jah*, we both wanted to see the beach. Shiloh said she'd never been."

A heavy sigh echoed through the phone, and Mikey got the feeling Silas wanted to wring his neck. "Let me talk to Shiloh."

He handed the phone to his *fraa* with a look of apology. "He wants to talk to you," Mikey whispered while covering the microphone.

"Hi, *Dat*." Shiloh smiled. "*Jah*, I'm fine."

She nodded and nibbled on her lip. "*Jah*, he's behaving himself."

Mikey grinned with mischief as his fingers glided over her shimmering skin. She pinned him with a warning look.

"I'm fine, *Dat*. Don't worry. Okay, I'll tell him." She smirked and shook her head. "I plan to go see you and *Mamm* when we get back. Okay, bye. Love you."

She ended the call and handed the phone back to him.

"What are you supposed to tell me?" Mikey beamed.

"To keep your hands off me." She giggled.

"Not a chance, *fraa*." He bent down and met her lips with his, then chuckled. "You said I was behaving, though. I didn't expect you to lie to your *dat*."

"*Ach*." She playfully swatted his arm. "I didn't lie. I said you were behaving yourself. And you are, just like a husband should." She punctuated her words with a cute curt nod.

He laughed and claimed another kiss. "*Ach*, woman, you make me all *ferhoodled*."

"The beach." Silas frowned at Kayla. "He took her. To. The. Beach."

"They're adults, remember?" Kayla reminded him, her comforting hand massaging his shoulder.

Silas's hand raked through his hair. "*Jah*, so were me and Josiah and our other friends when we went." He tilted his head at her. "And look how *that* turned out."

Kayla shifted his face to hers and studied him. "I think it turned out quite well, don't you?"

"*Ach*, that's not what I mean."

"I know. You're worried." She slipped her hand in his offering the reassurance he needed. "You've got to trust God, Silas. Put it in His hands."

"You're right. I just...I know boys, *nee*, men his age. I used to be one."

"This is something we can't control. We've done our part. We've raised Shiloh the best we know how. What more can we do?"

"*Jah*, you're right."

"God has a plan for her. For all of our children. I know it's hard to let go, but we have to. They're going to make their own mistakes, but they need to find their own way."

He looked at his *fraa* and smiled. "How'd you get so wise?"

Kayla shrugged. "Oh, I don't know. Hanging around my husband?"

He cupped her cheek and kissed her on the lips. "*Gott* was *gut* to give me you."

"He was good to both of us." To his delight, she returned his gentle kiss with passion.

TWELVE

Michael pitched a forkful of hay over the stall. *Dawdi* Sammy worked alongside him at a somewhat slower pace. He hated to admit it to himself, but *Dawdi* was getting older. Michael didn't even want to think about *Dawdi* passing on to glory and not being here. *Dawdi* had been the one constant throughout his entire life.

"What should we do about Mikey?" Michael stopped working and turned to *Dawdi*.

"We should continue to pray for him."

"*Jah*, I know that. But I don't like him being upset with you. He has no idea how much of a blessing you are."

"I'm glad you think of me that way." *Dawdi* chuckled and squeezed Michael's shoulder. "If I recall correctly, you haven't always thought of me as a blessing. You don't need to worry about Mikey. He'll come around in his own time. Just like his *vatter* did."

"I feel bad that he's taken Silas's *dochder* with him. I hate bearing the responsibility for that."

"You bear no responsibility where Mikey is concerned. He is a grown man and he'll make his own decisions."

"But what if they're the wrong decisions?"

"Then he'll have to live with the consequences."

Jah, that was what he was afraid of. How many consequences was Michael dealing with now because of his own *dumm* choices? Which reminded him...

"Uh, *Dawdi*, I need to go into town."

"You wantin' some company?"

"*Nee*. Not this time. Thanks for the offer, though." He glanced toward the house. "Would you let Miri know I'll be back before supper?"

Dawdi frowned. "You don't want to kiss your *fraa* goodbye?"

"*Nee*. She wasn't feeling *gut* this morning, so she's taking a nap. If you could just help her with the *kinner*, that would be *gut*."

Dawdi nodded, his thoughtful gaze probing.

"*Denki*."

Mikey reached for his *fraa's* hand as the two of them strolled along the shoreline, the cool ocean water lapping at their feet.

"I don't think I'm going to ever be able to return to normal life after this." Shiloh raised her face, basking in the sunshine. "This feels so *gut*."

"*Jah*, I know. I don't want to be away from you. Ever." Mikey slung his arm around her shoulders and claimed a kiss.

"Your *vatter* has family in Pennsylvania, right? Have you ever thought about visiting them?"

"That's a sore subject with *Dat*. I can't say I've ever thought about visiting, though." He glanced toward the water. "I do wonder about them and the whole situation with *Dat*."

"So, you've *never* met your grandparents?"

"Not on *Dat's* side."

"What about your *grossdawdi* Sammy? He doesn't talk to them, either?"

"I think he might. He sends off letters every now and then. I always figured it was probably to family in Pennsylvania."

"Aren't you curious? Don't you wonder what happened?"

"*Jah*, of course. But if *Dat* doesn't want to talk about it, that's his right."

"It just seems sad to me. I can't imagine not talking to my folks for the rest of my life, just brushing them off and pretending they don't exist. I mean, they're the ones who brought me into the world and cared for me all those years. They taught me so much." She shook her head.

"I'm sure he has a *gut* reason." He stopped walking and studied her. "What would you do? I mean, if you were me?"

"I think I'd try to find answers."

"How?"

Her steady eyes met his. "How far are we from Pennsylvania?"

THIRTEEN

"I can't believe I let you talk me into this." Mikey drummed his fingers on the steering wheel.

"And I still can't believe *you* talked me into leaving my folks. *And* marrying you."

Mikey grinned. "Smartest thing I ever did."

"I'm excited to go to Pennsylvania. Aren't you?"

"I'm just glad now that you talked me into going back to the trailer to grab our clothes before we left. Who knows how strict they are? They might not approve if I were to show up in *Englisch* clothes."

"Even though you're driving a car?"

"They'll figure I'm in *rumspringa*." He shrugged.

"Are you nervous?"

"Let's just say I have some concerns about meeting them."

"Afraid of what you'll find out?"

"Maybe."

"Well, look on the bright side. You'll be meeting your *mammi* and *dawdi* for the first time."

"Don't you think my *dat* probably had *gut* reason to walk away and never look back? I just don't know what we might be walking into. I mean, what if they hate me?"

"Why on earth would they hate *you*?"

He shrugged. "I don't know. I am my father's son."

"*Nee*. You are your own person. I didn't fall in love with your *vatter*, I fell in love with you." She lifted a half-smile. "Although I am glad he passed on his *gut* looks to you."

"*Jah*, me too." He raised his eyebrows twice and chuckled.

She shook a teasing finger at him. "But you shouldn't be *hochmut* about it."

"*Nee*. Of course, not." He attempted to suppress a smile.

Several hours later, they pulled into a white-fence-lined driveway. Trees on both sides created a shaded canopy from the road all the way to the fancy house.

"Wow! This looks really nice." Shiloh's mouth formed an O.

Mikey laughed. "I think they might be rich." He

hadn't realized the miles of white fence that surround this lush property belonged to his grandparents. Had his father grown up here?

"Are they *Englischers*?"

"Not that I know of. But then, I don't know much about them. Just that their names are Walter and Edna Eicher."

"This is..."

"Unexpected." Mikey nodded. "I'm guessing they must raise horses." He pointed to the sleek Arabians enclosed in a fence.

"Wow, that horse barn is huge!"

Mikey swallowed. "This is going to be awkward."

"*Nee*, it'll be fine. You are their *gross sohn*, after all."

"Right." He parked his car in front of what appeared to be a garage and took a deep breath. "Well, here goes nothin'."

"Mikey." Shiloh frowned. "Let's try to have a positive attitude about this, okay?"

"Okay, *Mamm*."

Shiloh shook her head. "Oh dear, now I sound like your *mamm*?"

"What should we call each other? Never mind, I'll just say you're my *schatzi*, which is totally true." He jumped out and went around to open the door for Shiloh. "I'm nervous."

"I know. Me too. Maybe we should pray."

"I think I'm too nervous to pray."

"Okay, I will." She bowed her head and whispered aloud, "Dear *Gott*, please let this be a *gut* visit. Amen."

"*Gut* enough." He sucked in a breath and held it.

Shiloh reached for his hand, and they walked up the fancy flowered pathway to the door. Shiloh knocked before he could turn around and change his mind.

The door flew open and an Amish woman, probably in her sixties, gasped. "Michael?" Shaky fingers flew to her mouth.

Was this his grandmother? He assumed she was, but...

Shiloh nudged him.

"I'm Mikey, Michael's oldest son."

Tears sprang to the woman's eyes. "*Ach. Jah*, of course. You would be his *sohn*."

He cleared his throat. "And you're...?"

"I'm Edna, your *mammi*." She raised a finger in the air. "Just a minute. Let me call your *dawdi* in. He'd want to be here."

She opened the door wide. "*Ach*, where are my manners? *Kumm* in, *kumm* in." *Mammi* Edna gestured toward a fancy living room area. "Have a seat while I go call your *dawdi* in and make us something to drink."

78

Mikey glanced at Shiloh, and she tilted her head toward the couch. "Let's sit down," she whispered.

"Can you *kumm* in right now? We have special company." *Mammi* Edna's voice carried as she spoke into a walkie talkie.

Mikey took in the room that looked way too elegant to be Amish. Yet, somehow, it was? The comfortable plush leather sofa he and Shiloh sat on, along with the pristine walnut coffee table and matching bookcase, screamed of wealth. His grandparents' Amish district must be *much* faster than both Detweiler's and Bontrager's, judging by the modern décor and gas lamps hanging from the ceiling. Not a lantern in sight.

A few moments later, *Mammi* Edna walked into the living room carrying a tray holding a glass pitcher with floating lemon slices inside and four tumblers. "I hope you like lemonade."

"*Jah*, we love it. *Grossdawdi* Sammy makes it all the time." At her signal, Mikey poured them each a tumblerful. He guessed *Grossdawdi* must've passed on his love of lemonade to his son, because this looked and tasted exactly like his.

Mammi Edna smiled. "It's your *Grossmammi* Bertie's recipe."

He nodded. "I never got to meet her."

"She owned your *grossdawdi's* heart." *Mammi* Edna seemed to be recalling a faraway memory, then she shot up when the back door creaked open. "That's your *dawdi*."

Mikey's eyes trailed *Mammi* Edna as she disappeared from the room. He blew out another long breath, unsure of how his grandfather would react to his presence. Fortunately, *Mammi* Edna had seemed pleased to meet him.

Shiloh's hand slipped into his, offering a moment of reassurance.

As soon as his *dawdi* walked into the room, Mikey could see the resemblance. He stood up and Shiloh followed suit.

Mammi Edna introduced them. "This is our Michael's *sohn* Mikey and his..."

Ach, he'd forgotten to introduce his *fraa*. He gestured to Shiloh. "And this is my *schatzi*, Shiloh. She's Silas Miller's *dochder*."

"I'm your *Dawdi* Walter, but most folks call me Walt."

"*Dawdi* Walt, then?"

"That sounds perfect." A pleased smile graced his lips. He looked down at his work clothes and grimaced. "I'd sit down and join you, but I probably shouldn't or your m*ammi* will have my hide."

"Why don't you take a quick shower and join us?"

Mammi Edna suggested. "That is, if Mikey and Shiloh can stay for a while."

"We plan to be in Pennsylvania until tomorrow," Mikey volunteered.

"Oh." *Mammi* Edna's eyes lit up. "Do you already have a place to stay?"

"*Nee*. We were going to figure that out after we left here."

"Well, why don't you stay here with us, then? We've got plenty of room in this place. I can just fix up a couple of rooms for the two of you."

"*Ach*, well, we'd only need one. Shiloh and I...well, we usually share a room," Mikey admitted. He ignored Shiloh's nudge. If he could get by without having to sleep separate from his *fraa*, then he would.

Both of his grandparents studied them momentarily, causing a blush to creep up Shiloh's cheeks.

"I see," *Mammi* said, sharing a look with *Dawdi*.

"But, if y'all aren't okay with that, then we don't have to." He sure hoped they didn't have any objections.

"And your folks are okay with this?" It was *Dawdi* this time.

"I haven't asked them." Mikey shrugged. "But Shiloh and I *do* live together in Indiana. We're in *rumspringa*." He glanced at his *fraa*, who looked like she wanted to bop him over the head with one of the books in *Mammi's* bookcase.

"I see," *Dawdi* said.

Mikey prattled on, "We *are* planning to have an Amish wedding this fall."

"That's *gut*." *Mammi's* hand covered her heart, and he recognized the relief in her tone.

"You're actually the first to hear about it, so please don't share the news with anyone." Not that they would. But if they did mention it to *Grossdawdi* Sammy in one of their letters, then it would no longer be a secret. And it could possibly get back to Shiloh's *vatter*. *Ach*, he shouldn't have opened his big mouth.

Mammi turned to *Dawdi*. "Walt, why don't you go get cleaned up so you can join us?"

Dawdi nodded. "I'll be back in a jiffy."

They all resumed their seating positions as *Dawdi* disappeared around a corner.

"I'm sorry, Shiloh. I didn't mean to embarrass you." Mikey grimaced, rubbing her knee.

She glanced at *Mammi* and then shrugged as if it were no big deal. "Well, we *do* live together."

But Mikey knew he'd disappointed her. He'd have to apologize later.

"Is there anything in particular you two would like for supper?" He was relieved when *Mammi* changed the subject.

"Anything sounds *gut* to me." Mikey smiled. "Shi?"

Shiloh's smile was easy. "*Jah*, I'm fine with whatever you'd like to serve. I'd be happy to help."

"Well, I was kind of thinking of ordering pizza if your *dawdi* is okay with that. Do you two like pizza?"

"I love pizza!" Mikey could taste it now.

"And Shiloh and I can throw a nice salad together to go with it," *Mammi* suggested.

"That sounds perfect." Shiloh clasped her hands in her lap.

"Well, let me go ahead and prepare that room for you." *Mammi* rose from her wingback chair.

"Actually, I think I'd be more comfortable with a separate room, if that's okay?"

Ach, why did Shiloh have to go and say that?

Mammi offered an understanding smile and nodded in pleasure.

Mikey frowned as his *mammi* left the room. "Why'd you say that?" he whispered.

"If someone back home finds out we stayed here, they might ask. It'll be better if we sleep in separate rooms, ain't not?" she whispered back.

"*Nee*, not for me!"

She wrinkled her nose and tweaked his earlobe. "You're so cute."

Mikey groaned in protest.

FOURTEEN

"So, what brings you two all the way out to Pennsylvania?" *Dawdi* Walt took a drink of his lemonade, eyeing Mikey and Shiloh from his recliner across the coffee table.

"Shiloh and I wanted to see the ocean, which we did. While we were there, the subject of y'all came up and we decided to take a detour before we headed back home." He shrugged. "Since I'd never met you, I thought it might be nice to. And maybe get some pieces to *mei vatter's* past."

"What has he shared with you?" *Dawdi's* dark brow arched.

"Pretty much nothing. I wouldn't even have known y'all's names if I hadn't seen it on *Grossdawdi* Sammy's mail."

Sadness blanketed both *Mammi* and *Dawdi's* faces. "That's a shame. But not completely unexpected."

"What happened between you?" His gazed ping-ponged between his grandparents. "I know *Dat* is never going to share anything with me."

"You've never asked your *grossdawdi* about it?"

"*Jah*, I have. He says it's not his story to tell." Mikey stared at his *dawdi*. "But it *is* yours."

"How old are you, Mikey?"

"Twenty-four. Why?"

"So, your *vatter* was, what? About nineteen when you were born?"

"I guess. I was adopted out and then my folks got me back when I was four." Mikey frowned. "My adoptive parents have passed away."

"That's right. I recall your *grossdawdi* mentioning that in his letters several years back. I'm sorry you had to go through that, *sohn*. If we'd known, we would have happily taken you in."

"*Dat* said he didn't even know about me when I was born. He was living in the world at that time."

"I see." *Dawdi* nodded. "But he eventually married your *mamm*, right? And they're still married?"

"They are." His forehead scrunched. "So, my father was an only child?"

"*Jah*. Your *mammi* had a difficult time when she was in the *familye* way with your *vatter*. We didn't want to chance possibly losing a *boppli* or your *mammi*. So, we learned to be content with our one."

And then they'd lost him.

"What happened to cause the rift between you and my *vatter*?" He needed to get to the heart of the matter before they spent all their time chitchatting. That had been the main reason he and Shiloh had come to Pennsylvania. He wanted answers.

Dawdi glanced at *Mammi*. "Are you ready for this?"

Mammi Edna sighed. "I think he has a right to know why we've been absent his entire life."

"You're right," *Dawdi* Walt agreed, then his gaze probed Mikey. "Your *vatter* was fifteen when he met an *Englisch* girl. She was fourteen at the time. Anyhow, they'd been dating in secret. When he was sixteen, he came to your *Mammi* and me and said he wanted to marry this *Englisch* girl."

"At sixteen?" Mikey's eyes widened.

"*Jah*. But since they were minors, they needed our permission. We'd have to sign papers okaying a union we did not approve of."

"I see."

"We didn't want him leaving the Amish. And he was too young for the responsibilities that come with marriage and being the head of a household, especially in the *Englisch* world where there is no support system."

"And so he left?"

Tears surfaced as *Dawdi* locked eyes with *Mammi*. "*Nee*. Not then."

"What happened then?"

"We insisted he put their relationship to an end. We encouraged him to join the Amish *youngie* so that he'd hopefully meet a *gut* Amish *maedel* and eventually settle down once he was older and more mature."

"And did he break it off with her?"

Again, *Dawdi* glanced at *Mammi*. "We think so. He became involved with the youth, but he was also getting himself into trouble. And then a few months later, he slammed through the door yelling and sobbing. He'd said it was all our fault."

"*What* was your fault?"

"The *Englisch* girl he'd broken up with had taken her own life. And she'd been expecting Michael's *boppli*. We don't think he knew about it until they found the note she'd left." *Dawdi* shoved away an avalanche of tears.

"*Ach*. That's terrible." Tears burned his own eyes.

"I can still hear him now. *She's gone! They're gone. You did this! You killed her. You killed them both.*" *Dawdi* looked at *Mammi* Edna, who's eyes shimmered with moisture. "We tried to talk to him, but he wouldn't hear it. He said there would *never* be anything that we could say to make this right. We *ruined* his life, he said, and he never wanted to see us again. And then, he stormed out the door and never spoke to either of us again."

"So, he hasn't seen or spoken to you once since then?"

He shook his head. "*Nee*. All our letters have returned to us unopened."

Mikey mulled over the tragic situation. "Well, you can't hardly blame him." Shiloh gasped at his blunt comment.

Dawdi Walt hung his head. "No, I don't."

Mammi refilled tumblers, her expression downcast. "We've been praying for him since the day he left. *Ach*, before that even. But more fervently since he left." She continued, "His life sort-of went into a downward spiral after that. He stayed with your *grossdawdi* for a while, then left the Amish for several years."

"*Jah*, that's when I came along," Mikey realized.

Dawdi reached for *Mammi's* hand. "It wasn't until his motorcycle accident and your *grossdawdi's* sage wisdom that he began opening his eyes. He's come a long way, according to your *grossdawdi*, but he still holds onto unforgiveness. He doesn't realize that the anger and bitterness is hurting him. His heart has been broken. *Gott* wants to heal Michael's heart, but he's got to let Him."

"And how does he do that?"

"By forgiveness. Forgiveness will set him free. There is a spot inside his heart that is closed up right now. Nobody can touch it—not even *Der Herr*. Not unless Michael allows Him to."

"I'm not sure he *can* forgive that. I think *I* would have a difficult time forgiving something of that magnitude. I mean, if it were Shiloh and me..." Mikey shook his head.

"Forgiveness may be easy for some. Not so easy for others. And our willingness to forgive depends on how much of our heart we want to let *Der Herr* own."

Anger stirred at the insinuation. "Are you saying *the devil* owns the other part?"

"The Bible is clear on this matter." *Dawdi* explained, "It says, *Be ye angry and sin not: Let not the sun go down upon your wrath.* Also, it says we are to put bitterness, anger, wrath—and all those other evil things that steal our peace—away from us. We are supposed to be tenderhearted and forgiving of each other. This is what *Der Herr* approves of, and what each of us should seek."

"I realize that, but forgiving at the drop of the hat isn't always easy."

"*Nee*, it's not easy for most of us. But it *can* be done if we do it in Christ's strength instead of our own. *I can do all things through Christ, which strengtheneth me, Gott's* Word says."

Mikey glanced at Shiloh, who lifted a half-smile and nodded in apparent agreement.

"Was there anything else you wanted to discuss?" *Dawdi* asked.

"So, you've never met *Mamm*, then."

"*Nee*. We, unfortunately, have not."

"Well, now that I've met you, I want to invite you to Shiloh's and my wedding." His eyes meandered to Shiloh for approval, and she nodded.

Dawdi blew out a breath. "That would please me and your *mammi* to no end, but I'm afraid your *vatter* will take issue with it."

"I know. But I have a plan." Mikey winked.

Everyone in the room turned their attention to him at the same time, and he chuckled. "I can't really divulge it now, but it will definitely involve your prayers, if you're willing."

"*Jah*, we are willing. For sure," *Mammi* Edna smiled now.

"Would you two like a tour of the ranch before supper?" Dawdi offered.

Mikey grinned at Shiloh. "I thought you'd never ask."

FIFTEEN

Mikey leaned forward to receive the warm hug his *mammi* offered.

"Thank you for coming by. You don't know how much this meant to us." When he pulled back, tears glistened in her eyes.

His *dawdi* embraced him also. "*Jah*, this gives us hope and something to look forward to."

"I'm glad Shiloh and I got to meet you." Mikey stood next to his vehicle. "Your place is amazing."

"*Jah*, it is." *Dawdi's* tone didn't hold much enthusiasm. "But with just your *mammi* and me, it's lonely."

Mikey glanced at Shiloh. "Maybe we can come visit again sometime after we're married in the Amish church."

"We'd like that."

They both slid into Mikey's car and waved a bittersweet goodbye.

"I like your grandparents," Shiloh turned to him once they pulled out onto the road.

"*Jah*, me too. They were a lot different than I expected."

"I'm glad we stopped by. I think it was a *gut* visit."

He released a long sigh. "*Jah*, it was. I just don't know what to do about my father."

"That's a sad situation. You know it hurt him deeply if he still hasn't gotten past it after all these years."

"*Jah*. I'm pretty sure not even *mei mamm* knows about it." He shook his head. "To think I have an older *bruder* or *schweschder* in Heaven…"

"It's kind of sad to think about now, but have you ever pondered Heaven and what a happy place it's going to be?"

Mikey frowned. "Do you think my *bruder* or *schweschder's mamm* is there? I mean, if she took her own life. That's like murdering yourself. And then, there was the *boppli* too."

"I think it's possible. I mean, according to what *Dat* has said, suicide isn't an automatic going to hell offense. It all depends on if a person knows Jesus or not."

"*Jah*, but the Bible says that no murderer has eternal life abiding in them. So, how does that work?"

"Well, it also says that there is no condemnation for those who are in Christ. If you're *in* Christ, that means you've believed on Him for salvation. There's no condemnation because *Gott* has already washed all your sins away."

"I know all that, but what if you sin right before you die? You can't repent of that."

"So, you think that after you have trusted Jesus, you have to be perfect and sinless? *Nee*, that's why we need Jesus in the first place. We *can't* be perfect, but He is. That's why the Bible says those who are *in* Christ. When you stand before *Der Herr* at the judgment, you are standing in Christ, which means you are pure, clean, and holy. His grace is covering you. You will have no sin in you because Jesus has taken care of it."

"I see. I think." He chuckled.

"The Bible also puts it this way. It says that we are sealed with the Holy Spirit unto the day of redemption. Something that is sealed is safe and secure and official. That's what Jesus does for us. And that's why we can have peace, because we know we are safe in Him."

His mouth opened and he stared at her. "You know what I think?"

"What?"

"I think I married the smartest woman alive."

Shiloh laughed. "I think you might be a little bit *ab im kopp*."

"You're probably right, but so am I." He winked.

She glanced out the window as he turned onto the freeway. "Are you going to be ready to face *mei dat* when we get back home?"

"I'll be ready for anything after a *gut* night's sleep with my *fraa* by my side."

She pulled her bottom lip between her teeth and smiled shyly. "I love falling asleep in your arms. I'm going to miss it when we move back home to join the *G'may*."

"I'll be counting down the days till our wedding for sure and certain. I'm just glad that we'll have spring and summer together before we have to go back to the Amish."

"I still want to go to church and all that. You don't mind, do you?" Her eyes searched his.

"People are going to judge us, you know. Because we're living together. They'll probably preach on it too."

"It doesn't bother me. Besides, we're married now. I have no reason to feel guilty."

"*Jah*, I guess you're right." He shrugged.

A smile slipped from Shiloh's mouth as she and Mikey pulled up to her folks' house. She loved living with Mikey in their little rented trailer, but this was the place that felt like home. Maybe because she'd been born and raised here or because of the familiarity of an Amish farm. Whatever it was about this property just brought a sense of peace.

"Shiloh!" Sierra squealed and ran to meet her the moment she stepped from Mikey's car.

Shiloh laughed and engulfed her younger *schweschder* in a hug. "Missed me, huh?"

"You have no idea how much. Judah has been driving me crazy." She rolled her eyes.

"I believe you."

"*Mamm* said you and Mikey went to the coast? Lucky duck."

"*Jah*, it was really nice. You have to see it someday." Shiloh dug into her purse. "Here, I got you a souvenir."

Sierra held the cute keychain in her hand. "It's a sea turtle!"

"The minute I saw it I knew I had to get it for you." Shiloh couldn't suppress her smile. She had been certain Sierra would love it.

"*Denki*, Shi. I'll use it for my store and house keys."

Mikey cleared his throat.

"Oh, sorry to ignore you, Mikey," Sierra said. "Did you have a *gut* time at the coast too?"

"Oh, yeah." He raised his eyebrows and winked at Shiloh.

"*Shiloh*?" Sierra's voice held caution. "What does he mean by *that*?"

"He's just messing with you." Shiloh recovered.

"I see the pink on your cheeks." Sierra accused.

Shiloh threw an arm around Sierra. "*Schweschder*, there are times when you don't want to share all your secrets."

"You are going to be in so much trouble."

"Mikey and I have done absolutely nothing wrong." Okay, so maybe that wasn't entirely true. They were secretly married.

Mikey coughed, drawing Sierra's attention.

"Don't mind him. He's just trying to stir the pot." Shiloh shot Mikey a look of warning. "You behave."

"Always." Mikey smirked and raised his eyebrows twice.

Shiloh ignored the little instigator. "I'm here to get my soapmaking supplies. I'll be bored to tears if I have nothing to do all day."

"*Jah*, she needs to make more of her kissing soap." Mikey teased.

Sierra's eyes widened. "Kissing soap?"

98

Shiloh shook a finger at her husband. "You. You're trouble, you know that?"

"I like trouble." Mikey insisted.

A throat cleared behind Mikey and he turned to see *Dat* standing there, arms crossed over his chest.

"*Ach*, Silas." Mikey tossed a *thanks for the warning* look at Shiloh.

Sierra laughed. "Now, you're in trouble."

"Trouble for what?" *Dat* said.

Shiloh shook her head. "He was just teasing Sierra, is all."

"Well, either way, we're glad to have you back home." *Dat* tugged her to his side for a hug. "Even if it is just for supper. *Kumm* into the house. *Mamm* will be happy to see you."

"*Ach*, I haven't even been gone a whole week yet."

"Which should show you how much you're missed." He glanced toward Mikey. "*Kumm* on, Mikey. We'll let you come inside too." *Dat* teased.

Mikey had been right, Shiloh realized. This wasn't much different than them being married in the Amish church and visiting. Even so, Shiloh couldn't wait for the day when she could share their plans to marry in the fall with *Mamm* and *Dat*. They would be so pleased.

At least, she *hoped* they would approve.

SIXTEEN

While Mikey enjoyed his honeymoon and the time he'd been spending with Shiloh, it was nice to get back to work at the feedstore. Between his stint in jail and his time off, it had been three weeks since he'd worked, and the funds he had saved up were dwindling quickly. Not to mention, he was starting to feel lazy.

The feedstore didn't pay all that much, though, so it would be great if he could find a side job that brought in a little extra cash. He'd definitely need it now that he was living away from his *grossdawdi's* farm and providing for Shiloh as well.

"It's good to have you back, Mikey." Jeff, his middle-aged manager, grinned. "Customers have been asking about you."

His brow shot up. "They have?"

Jeff nodded. "One woman, in particular."

Mikey groaned. *Not her.* He didn't even want to think about the racy *Englisch* woman ten years his senior that somehow always needed his "help."

"Yep. *Where's that hot Amish guy that usually works here?*" Jeff said in his best female voice.

"You're kidding. Hopefully you told her I quit and was never coming back?" Wishful thinking.

Jeff chuckled. "You know I don't twist the truth. I did say that I didn't know when you were coming back, though, so maybe that will buy you a little time."

"One can only hope."

"She has been coming in rather frequently, so I thought I'd give you fair warning."

"Thanks for the heads-up." He slipped the box cutter out of his pocket and opened the case of flea collars that needed to be restocked.

Jeff eyed him from the cash register, inventory clipboard in hand. "Heard a rumor you moved out and are living with an Amish girl."

Mikey couldn't suppress his smile if he wanted to. "It's true."

"I didn't know that kind of thing was allowed in the Amish religion." Jeff's head tilted.

"Neither of us have been baptized yet. And yes, it is frowned upon."

"So, you're not like shunned or anything?"

"Well, I'm sure the leaders in my district aren't happy with me since I'm dating a girl from the neighboring district." Mikey shook his head. "I don't know why Detweiler's made that *dumm* rule, anyhow."

"So, you can't just date any Amish woman? It must be someone from your own group?"

"*Jah*. But her district doesn't forbid her from seeing me."

Jeff shook his head. "I don't know if I could ever keep up with all those Amish rules."

"That makes two of us." Mikey chuckled.

"By the way, the owner gave you a raise."

"He did? Wow, that was unexpected. Tell him thank you for me, will you?" He'd actually never even met the owner of the store and assumed he must live far away. "Oh, my uh, girl wanted me to ask you if we could carry her soaps in here. She makes all kinds, but she thought the ones specially formulated for animals might sell well here. They're all natural and all that."

"I don't see why not. We could try it on consignment."

Mikey grinned, thinking of Shiloh's reaction. "Okay, thanks. I'll let her know."

Mikey dug into the delicious supper Shiloh had prepared for the two of them. Since it had been such a beautiful day, they'd opted to eat outside on the porch glider. "Guess what, Shi? I talked to Jeff at the feedstore today. He said they could take some of your soaps on consignment."

Just as he thought, her eyes lit up at the prospect. "Really? I better get busy, then. I'll have to make up a fresh batch tomorrow."

"Oh, and I was going to tell you. Jeff needs me to stay late a couple of nights this week. We're supposed to get some new inventory in. I figured I can leave the phone here with you during the day, since we have a phone at the store. That way, I can call and let you know."

"That's fine."

"I'm not sure how late I'll be so you don't need to make me supper or wait up for me."

Shiloh frowned, clearly not approving of the idea.

"I know. I don't like it either. But frankly, we can use the extra money. And I feel bad since I've been off for three weeks."

She acceded with an understanding nod. "I was hoping you could drop me off at my folks' place before you go to work on Friday. Since we don't have a washer here, I'll need to use *Mamm's*. If I go in the morning, I can get that done and help my folks if they need it. And then when you get off work, we can eat supper with *Mamm* and *Dat* before we go home."

"That sounds *gut*. I like that idea."

"I thought you would."

He gestured to the firepit. "But I still want to have a fire out here and roast marshmallows one of these nights."

"What if we invited some people over to hang out by the fire and play games and whatnot? Maybe Sierra and Judah?"

"*Jah*, we can do that sometime. What do you think about the two of us sleeping out under the stars one night in the summer?" Excitement pounded in his chest at the romantic notion.

"Like in a tent?"

"*Nee*, I was just thinking out in the open."

"We'll have to see how bad the mosquitos and other bugs are."

"You're right. I didn't think of that. The mosquitos could be bad with the pond not too far away."

"If we were to get one of those tents with the mesh on top, we could still be outside and see the stars."

"That might be a plan." Mikey sighed in contentment. "You know, I'm going to miss living out here on our own after we go back to the Amish."

"*Jah*, but we're getting married. We can do whatever we want after that. We could buy something like this ourselves, right?"

"*Ach*, that would be a dream for sure."

She stared off toward the woods, likely dreaming with him. "Do you think your *mammi* and *dawdi* will come to our wedding?"

"I hope so. I need to talk to *mei dat*." He blew out a breath. "I just need to figure out what to say. I'm not sure how to approach the subject."

"So, since we're getting married again, does this mean we get to go on another honeymoon?" She teased.

"If we can afford it, I'd love to." He turned to her, searching her facial features. "What do you think of me getting a second job?"

Her face crumpled. "I already have a feeling I'm going to get awfully lonely with you gone working every day. And then, you just said you are going to work overtime..." Her chin trembled.

Ach. He reached for her hand and enclosed her fingers in his. "*Nee*, I was thinking here at home. I've fixed a few lawnmowers for the *Englisch* when I lived at home with *Dat,* and we did some tractor work too. He used to work at an *Englisch* mechanic shop, so he taught me some things. Anyway, I could put up some fliers around town."

"I would like that a lot better than you being gone all the time." Her nod of approval eased some of his anxiety. The last thing he wanted was a lonely wife longing for something else.

"It suits me. I think that's what I'd like to do after we're married. Maybe open up a shop." He set their empty plates to the side.

"I think that's a *gut* idea. I like the thought of having you home all the time."

"I'd probably be pretty busy, of course, but at least I'd be there on our property. When we get some, that is."

"Do we have extra money for me to hire a driver? I'd like to go into town one day and go shopping, if that's okay with you."

"You know I'd give you a bucket full of stars if you asked for them and it was in my power to do it." He leaned close and kissed her lips. "I'm so glad I get to do forever with you."

SEVENTEEN

Life was an interesting thing, Mikey pondered.

Somehow, between his marriage to Shiloh and meeting his paternal grandparents, the anger he'd felt toward *Grossdawdi Sammy* had melted away. Before, he'd been so angry he could hardly see straight, but now he had a new appreciation for his elders.

If he could pinpoint the moment his icy heart began thawing, he'd probably go back to the conversation he'd had with *Dawdi* and *Mammi* Eicher. *Dawdi* Walt's words on forgiveness had struck like an arrow straight into his heart.

Now that he thought about *Dawdi* Walt, he wondered if he might be one of the leaders in his Amish district. Mikey hadn't thought to ask at the time, but now he was curious. He'd have to ask *Grossdawdi* Sammy about that.

He breathed a silent prayer for wisdom as he pulled

up to *Grossdawdi's* farm. He'd have to do some pretending today, whether he liked it or not. Because if he had any hope of *Dat* opening up about the past, he'd need to let him know that he identified with him—and he did, even though he'd already released his own bitterness to *Der Herr*.

Yikes, had it really been over three weeks since he'd last come home? As soon as he opened the car door, *Dat* neared him with purposeful strides.

"Has the prodigal returned?" *Dat's* gaze was hopeful.

Mikey grimaced. "Not exactly."

"I heard you sweet-talked Silas Miller's *dochder* into moving in with you. Is that true?" *Dat's* arms crossed over his chest.

Heat crept up his neck. "*Jah*, it's true."

"Silas wasn't too happy about it." *Dat* frowned.

"*Jah*, I know." Mikey stared at his boots.

"I'm assuming you're going to do the *right* thing and marry her?"

"You assume correctly. We eventually want to get married in the Amish church. Jerry Bontrager's."

"And until then, you're just..." *Dat's* wrist turned a circle.

"You know how it is."

Dat gave a hard nod. "*Jah*, unfortunately, I do. It's

not a path I would recommend."

"*Dat*, I'm an adult and so is Shiloh."

"I realize that. But wisdom isn't a respecter of age." His gaze was pointed. "And living in sin is never wise."

"*Jah*." Mikey rubbed the back of his neck. "Can we talk about something else now?"

"It's your call, sohn."

"I was hoping to talk to you about maybe starting my own business. After Shiloh and I get hitched in the Amish church, I'd like to open a small engine shop."

Dat grinned and Mikey sensed pride in his demeanor. "That's because it's in your blood. You're a natural at it."

"*Jah*, but how do I start a business doing that?"

"You do a good job and charge a fair price. Word will get out and you'll get more customers than you know what to do with."

"That's *gut* to know." Anticipation filled him at the thought of being able to provide for Shiloh apart from the feedstore.

"I have news you might be interested in." *Dat* smirked.

Mikey lifted an eyebrow.

"We had a meeting last week. They voted to lift the ban on mixing with Bontrager's district."

"What?"

"They figured that a lot of the young folks were already mingling, and a wider gene pool is a *gut* thing." *Dat* shrugged. "You're free to court and marry Shiloh now without going against the *Ordnung*."

"*Ach*, Shiloh will be thrilled to hear this news."

"That means you won't have to worry about the *bann* either."

"That's *gut*. It was a bad rule from the beginning, in my opinion." Mikey glanced toward the barn. Time to step on the stage. He summoned his best scowl. "Is Sammy around?"

"*Sammy*? You mean *Grossdawdi*?"

"*Jah*, whatever." *Ach*, he was *gut* at playing the rebellious *sohn*.

"Oh, no. You are *not* going there. This is your *grossdawdi's* property and you will respect him. I don't care how angry you are with him about going to jail." Wow, he could almost see steam coming off *Dat's* head. *Gut*.

"Why should I?" He challenged.

"Because. It's the *right* thing to do. You need to forgive him if you feel he was wrong."

Bingo.

"Why should I forgive him?" Mikey crossed his arms across his chest.

"I just told you why."

112

"So, you want me to do something *you're* not willing to do?"

Dat's frown deepened. "What are you talking about, *sohn*?"

"I'm talking about your folks. *Mammi* and *Dawdi* Eicher. How come they've never come here to meet our family?"

"They're not welcome here."

"Why not?"

"This conversation isn't about them. It's about you and *Grossdawdi* Sammy."

"Well, maybe it's time to talk about them. It's hypocritical for you to expect me to just forgive *Grossdawdi* when you refuse to deal with your own past."

"What? Where is this coming from?" *Ach*, but *Dat* was angry. "And you have *no* idea about my past!" *Dat* pointed a finger in his chest.

"Why don't you talk about it, then?"

"As far as I'm concerned, your *dawdi* and *mammi* Eicher are dead. And buried is where they are going to stay." With that, *Dat* stomped off toward the fields, forcefully kicking a rock with his boot in the process.

Ach, that had gone worse than he thought. *Jah*, he needed to pray for *Dat*.

As soon as *Dat* was out of sight, Mikey slipped into the house. "*Mamm*?" he called out.

"Mikey, is that you?" She charged into the room, wiping her hands on her apron, then engulfed him in a hug.

Mikey chuckled. "Did you miss me?"

"More than you know." She gestured to the door. "What was your *dat* hollering for?"

"*Jah*, that's what I wanted to talk to you about." He frowned. "*Dat's* not happy."

"What happened?"

"It's kind of a long story. What do you know about his folks?"

"Pretty much nothing. It's something he's never really opened up about. All I know is they don't get along." *Mamm* gestured toward the table and they both sat.

"You never asked why?"

"I did. But your *vatter* is so closed about the subject. I did ask your *grossdawdi* about it, though."

"And what did he say? Because he told me it wasn't his story to tell."

"He told me a little bit about the situation."

"Can you keep a secret?"

Mamm's brow lowered. "From whom?"

"Everyone."

"That depends on what it's about."

"It's about *Dat* and his folks. I know what happened." He admitted.

"You do?" She frowned. "How?"

"You can't tell *Dat*. He'll be upset." He glanced toward the door to make sure no one was around. "Where are the *kinner*?"

"School and outside with Sammy. Except for the *boppli*."

He took a deep breath. "Shiloh and I visited *Mammi* and *Dawdi* Eicher in Pennsylvania."

EIGHTEEN

Michael passed *Dawdi* Sammy and the *kinner* on the way out to the field and sputtered a warning. "You might not want to go to the house right now. Mikey's home and he's in rare form today."

Dawdi's brow arched. "How so?"

"You'll see. You might want to steer clear of him. That's all I'm saying." Michael's two-year-old son lifted his arms and he picked him up and planted a kiss on his cheek.

Dawdi studied Michael. "You going somewhere?"

"Just for a walk. I need some air."

"I see."

Michael handed the little one to *Dawdi*, who placed him on the ground and took his hand. "I'll be back inside later."

"You don't want to see your *sohn*?" *Dawdi's* lips turned down.

"We've already had our talk. I just need some space right now."

"Okay. The little ones and I are about due for a drink, anyhow."

Michael watched *Dawdi* walk off. He'd been amazed that they'd had such a *gut* relationship all these years. It was something he'd definitely needed given the nonexistent relationship with his folks, whom he did not want to think about right now.

Why did Mikey have to bring them up all of a sudden? How long had it been since he'd given his folks even a passing thought?

He scowled. They weren't worth a passing thought. As far as he was concerned, his parents were as *gut* as murderers. And he didn't want murderers anywhere near his *fraa* or his *kinner*.

Ever.

Mamm listened quietly to Mikey as he told her everything that happened in Pennsylvania. Neither of them escaped the conversation with a dry eye.

"Your *vatter* hides his hurts well. I'm not sure what I can do to help the situation, though."

"I just want you to pray." He briefly touched her hand. "Can you keep another secret?"

"Wow. You're full of secrets today, aren't you?" *Mamm* smiled.

"Shiloh and I are planning to marry this fall in Bontrager's district."

Mamm's smile widened. "*Ach*, Mikey! I'm so happy for you."

"*Jah*, we are too. But *Mamm*, we want *Dawdi* Walt and *Mammi* Edna to come to our wedding."

"Oh dear." *Mamm* frowned now.

"I know. That's why I want us all to pray about it. Or, one of the reasons, at least." He swallowed. "But you can't tell anyone about our plans, okay? Or about *Mammi* and *Dawdi*."

"You have my word, *sohn*."

Their attention moved toward the door as *Grossdawdi* Sammy and the *kinner* tromped into the house.

"I hope your *mamm's* got some lemonade ready, because I know you're awfully thirsty," *Grossdawdi* said the words to the *kinner*, but they were purposely loud enough for *Mamm* to hear.

As they entered the kitchen, *Grossdawdi's* and Mikey's eyes met and held. Mikey swallowed. "Can we talk?"

Grossdawdi nodded. "Let me *chust* get a glass of cool lemonade and I'll join you out on the porch."

Mikey agreed and headed outside.

"*Kumm* back in to say goodbye before you go, *sohn*," *Mamm* called after him.

"I will." He smiled to himself as he sank onto the porch swing.

A moment later, *Grossdawdi* joined him.

"You have something you'd like to say?" Caution reflected in *Grossdawdi's* eyes.

"*Jah*. I thought you'd like to know that I'm not harboring any anger toward you, anymore."

Grossdawdi's head dipped. "That's *gut*."

"I know you probably had *gut* reason to do what you did. Although I'm not sure what your reasons were." He spoke honestly.

"I was your age once. It was a long time ago, but I remember it like yesterday."

He waited for *Grossdawdi* to continue.

"I too was on the wrong path and spent some time in jail."

His eyes widened. He hadn't expected such a confession from *Grossdawdi* Sammy.

"Seems it took many of my *vatter's* prayers and the love of a *gut* woman to screw my head on straight." *Grossdawdi* studied him.

"*Grossmammi* Bertie, right?"

Grossdawdi nodded. "But my time in jail gave me

time to ponder the path my feet were on and prove to me that there were consequences for my behavior."

"I see."

"I thought that maybe if you went to jail for a short time, you might gain the same wisdom I did." *Grossdawdi* shrugged.

"Well, I certainly don't want to go back in there. I plan to do everything I can to avoid it."

"*Gut*. I'm glad to hear that."

"I admit that I knew it was wrong, but I never thought carving my initials into a piece of wood would land me in jail."

"It's all about the location. There are a thousand trees you could have chosen in our woods, and no one would have cared a lick. But when it comes to government property, vandalism can be a big deal."

"*Grossdawdi*, I need to ask you something."

"Ask away."

"What can we do to help *Dat* restore his relationship with *Dawdi* and *Mammi* Eicher?"

Grossdawdi leaned back and stared at him. "What do you know about that?"

"I met them."

"Where?"

"In Pennsylvania. Shiloh and I went and visited them. They told me what happened with *Dat*." Mikey frowned. "I feel so bad about all of it."

"*Jah*, it's a sad situation for sure. I've encouraged your *vatter* to make amends. I'm not sure he ever will this side of Heaven." *Grossdawdi* released a heavy sigh.

"Me and *Mamm* and Shiloh are praying for him. Will you join us?"

"*Ach*, it's something I've been praying about for a very long time. Perhaps with more voices raising to *Gott*, we'll see the mountain begin to move. But I think this situation might take a bit more than that."

"What do you mean?"

"I'm talking about fasting."

"Like we do for Christmas and other special days?"

"Yes and no. I'm referring to a fast that lasts a little longer than a meal."

"How long?"

"Well, that would be between you and *Der Herr*."

"What if we chose one day a week and we *all* fasted and prayed that day?"

"I think that's a *gut* idea."

Mikey stood from the porch swing. "Well, I should probably get going or Shiloh might start to worry. And between you and me, *Dat* still thinks I'm angry with you." He shrugged. "I thought maybe if he gave me advice to reconcile with you, then an opportunity would come up to talk about his folks."

"And did it?"

"*Jah*, but the situation is worse than I thought. *Dat* totally blames them for his ex-girlfriend's death. I think he sees them as guilty as the person in the paper last week who was on trial for murder."

"I think there's more to it than that, *sohn*."

Mikey frowned. "What do you mean?"

"I think he may blame himself, but he's not willing to own up to it."

"I never thought of that, but you could be right."

"We have a lot to pray about. But if anyone can turn a heart around, *Gott* can. Your *vatter* has already come a long way."

"I know."

"I think it would be best not to mention anything to him at all. Let's *chust* pray, *jah*?"

"Do you think he'd revert back to his old ways?"

"I pray not. That's the last thing he needs."

NINETEEN

As Mikey stood at the hardware store counter, his mind wandered back to everything that had happened in his life in just a short amount of time. From getting caught at the covered bridge, to his time in jail, to finding himself and Shiloh a place to live, to convincing Shiloh to move in with him, to talking her into marrying him among the *Englisch* and their secret wedding and honeymoon at the beach, to meeting his grandparents for the first time and learning about his *vatter's* past, to his and Shiloh's plans to marry in the fall.

Ach, who would have guessed his life would become this crazy?

The bell above the door jingled.

"I see my favorite employee is back at work." An annoying female voice spoke way louder than necessary.

Oh no.

His eyes searched for his manager, who appeared to be busy outside with a customer. *Great. Just great.*

He sighed. Like it or not, he'd have to help this woman with whatever she needed. "May I help you?"

When she walked straight up to the counter, he was thankful for the barrier between them. Her finger dangled on her brightly colored pink lips, then her eyes widened. "Oh look! You have something right there."

Before he knew it, her hand was stroking the collar of his shirt.

He quickly pulled back. "I can get it," he insisted, brushing off whatever she'd been referring to.

"What do you say the two of us go out to dinner tonight?"

Ach, this woman was bold even for an *Englischer.*

"No, thank you."

"Come on. Now, I know by looking at your gorgeous face that you're not married, otherwise you'd have a beard."

"I already have a girl." He cleared his throat. "Did you need something from the store? We have some nice pet soap. It's *gut* stuff. All natural." He pointed to the new display of his *fraa's* soap offerings.

"Oh, yes. Silly me. I must've gotten distracted by those eyes." She giggled. "I'll take a couple of those soaps and..." She glanced around the store and twisted her lips. "Dog food. I'll need help with it."

Of course, she would. Mikey felt like rolling his "distracting" eyes.

"I'd like one of those ten-pound bags of dog food. Could you carry it out to my car for me?"

She couldn't carry out ten pounds? He shook his head.

"I would do it myself, but I just had these nails done." She tapped her nails on the counter while he rang up her purchase, then made sure to brush his fingers as she handed over her cash.

This must've been the strange woman Solomon warned about in Proverbs, he mused. Instead of grunting, he attempted an unaffected smile and thanked her for her business.

A few moments later, he effortlessly picked up the bag she could have easily lifted herself. "Sure. Just show me which vehicle is yours."

"It's the white SUV."

He walked outside to the vehicle she'd pointed to. The sooner he got her on her way, the better. "Where do you want it?"

"Just on the passenger's side is fine."

He deposited the bag on the floorboard, then startled when he turned around and came face to face with the woman. "*Ach*, excuse me."

Sheesh! He scurried back into the store as quickly as possible. Onlookers might have thought he was trying for the Olympic gold medal in running.

Jeff chuckled as Mikey blew out a breath once he was safely inside the store.

"Remind me why I work here again." His hand clenched the door knob behind him.

Jeff rubbed his fingers together.

"Oh, right. A paycheck." Mikey pointed out the window to the vehicle driving away. "Did you see that woman? She's crazy."

"Oh, I saw her, alright." He shook his head. "Don't forget we've got that delivery coming in today."

"Right. I need to call home and remind Shiloh."

Jeff grinned. "You and your girlfriend pretty serious, then?"

"*Jah.*"

"Any wedding bells in your future?"

"Amish don't have wedding bells. And if we get hitched, I'll be sure to get you an invitation."

"That's cool. Can I bring a plus-one?"

Mikey frowned. "A what?"

"That means my wife." Jeff smiled.

"*Ach*, *jah*. Sure." He picked up the phone. "Hey, Shi. I just wanted to remind you I need to stay late tonight. *Jah*. Don't wait for me."

TWENTY

S hiloh was grateful to be out and about today, especially since Mikey would be working late again tonight.

Since their trailer was so small, there was only so much time she could spend keeping house. And with a couple of soap-making days behind her, she'd made enough to sell at her folks' store and at the feedstore where Mikey worked.

Maybe she should take up another activity that could bring in a little money. She'd always enjoyed making candles, so maybe she'd add that to her soap offerings. Or basket weaving, maybe?

She briefly wondered how the landlord would feel if she were to cultivate a garden beside the trailer. At least then she could go out and pull weeds and have a harvest to put up later. But then, where would she put her canning jars? At *Mamm's*?

For sure, she'd need to find something to occupy her time, because after flipping through the channels on the television, she had no desire to watch any of the ridiculous shows. Perhaps she should stop by the library and borrow some *gut* books.

She'd mention it to the driver once she finished up her shopping. And maybe she would treat herself to a special drink at the little café in town. The thought put a smile on her face.

An hour later, her driver pulled up to the café and Shiloh hopped out. "I shouldn't be long." She informed her driver before waltzing inside the cozy establishment.

She ordered her fancy overpriced drink, then took a seat by the window while she waited for the worker to prepare it. *Ach.* She frowned as a couple sitting at a picnic bench at the park across the street appeared to be conversing. She recognized the man—Mikey's *vatter*. But what was he doing and who was he having lunch with? Not that it was any of her business, of course.

Shiloh's mouth opened when the woman reached across the table and placed her hand over her father-in-law's. *Oh dear.*

Just then, her name was called from the coffee counter. She picked up her drink, then glanced toward the park as she entered her driver's car. Michael Eicher and his companion were no longer seated at the table, but strode toward a nearby car together.

The entire way home, a feeling of dread consumed Shiloh's gut. She didn't want to assume the worst, but what could be the explanation? Surely, there had to be a logical reason Mikey's father was sharing a meal with an *Englisch* woman he was not married to.

Ach, what should she say to Mikey? Or maybe she shouldn't say anything at all. No need to worry him when he had so many other things on his mind already.

She suppressed a groan. Perhaps she should have stayed home today after all.

Michael's hands plowed through his hair as he glanced down at the numbers on the paper in front of him. How on earth was he going to pay all this back child support? Miri had wanted him to stay at home to help with the *kinner*, but the income from *Dawdi's* farm was no longer enough to make ends meet. Not with these payments on top of their day-to-day living expenses.

Did the courts think he was rich? Raising his other

kinner hadn't cost anywhere near the amount that now threatened to swallow him whole.

He'd only met his *Englisch* sohn, Maddox, once. Fortunately, he'd shared the discovery with Miri years ago when he'd first found out. Keeping secrets from her was something he didn't want to get into the habit of doing. He already had enough skeletons in his closet.

Miri hadn't been surprised in the least, given his lifestyle and the reckless choices he'd made prior to their marriage. The Biblical law of sowing and reaping was manifesting itself in full force. Why had he been such an idiot in his younger days?

There were no two ways about it. He was going to have to take up a *gut*-paying job. Maybe he could get hired on at one of the local steel plants working the graveyard shift. That way, he would still be home during the day to help Miri out.

Either way, he had to find some way to pay his debts.

TWENTY-ONE

"I'm so happy to have you home, Shi. Even if it is just to do laundry." Sierra beamed as she handed Shiloh a pair of Mikey's wet work trousers.

Shiloh sent the pair through the wringer and they fell into the rinse bin. Then she did the same with the next items.

Their voices echoed in the basement as they chattered on about what had been happening since Shiloh had left. There had been several things she couldn't share with her *schweschder*, even though they were best friends.

"I still can't believe you and Mikey are living under the same roof. Let me tell you that there has been quite a bit of gossip about you two at the young folks' gatherings."

Jah, she figured there would be.

"Lucy was disappointed you didn't show up at the singing she and Justin hosted."

"*Jah*, I know. Mikey and I were at the beach that week."

"Must be nice."

Shiloh frowned. "In some ways, I suppose it is. But truthfully, I'm by myself most of the time and Mikey's off at work."

"I thought you said he was going to be working at home."

"That's what I'm hoping for. But he needs to find some customers first." She hefted the basket of damp clothes as soon as they'd completed their task. "Time to get these up on the line, ain't not?"

"The spring sunshine will feel nice after being in this basement."

Shiloh couldn't get over how much she'd missed her childhood home. Maybe Sierra would want to drive the buggy down to Lucy's for a visit.

"Uh-oh." Sierra held up a shirt. "Lipstick on Mikey's collar? Have you been testing out makeup again?"

"What? *Nee*." She grasped the shirt from her *schweschder* then examined it. She couldn't remember the last time she'd worn lip color. Not that her lips hadn't been on her husband's neck.

"Mm-hm." Sierra clearly didn't believe her. "I'm not sure you two living alone together is such a *gut* thing, *schweschder*."

Even if she did wear a little lip tint, it wouldn't be that bold of a color. She frowned at the shirt as she stared at it. How on earth could this color lipstick...?

She thought of Mikey's work schedule as of late. He'd been "working" after hours many nights this week, he'd said. And then he'd been too exhausted for anything intimate. *Ach. Nee.*

She didn't want to believe the worst, but...

Her mind flew back to earlier in the week when she'd seen Mikey's *dat* with another woman, then she recalled the conversation with his grandparents in Pennsylvania about his father's past, and then, of course, there was Mikey himself who'd been born out-of-wedlock.

Like it or not, there was a pattern. Was Mikey walking along a similar path as his father? Was that what *Dat* had meant when he'd said Mikey was *just like his father*?

Twin droplets of moisture trailed her cheek.

"Shiloh, what's wrong?"

"I think Mikey might be cheating on me!" She threw the shirt on the ground and ran to the safety of her old bedroom.

A moment later, Sierra's hand massaged Shiloh's

back as she sobbed into her pillow. "Shi, you don't know that. There could be a perfectly logical explanation for the lipstick. Maybe...maybe it's not even lipstick. It could be paint."

"Paint? In passion pink?" her voice screeched.

"The point is you don't know for sure. You should give him the benefit of the doubt."

"Right. Okay. I'm just overreacting, ain't not?"

"Now, sit up and take a deep breath and give me a hug." Sierra opened her arms, but Shiloh couldn't help it when the tears fell unbidden. Sierra mopped up her worry with a hankie.

"Enough of that. Now, do you have any news for me?"

"Well, you already know that Detweiler's lifted the courting restriction between our districts, ain't so?"

"What?" Sierra shot backward and examined her *schweschder*. "You're kidding, right?"

Shiloh shook her head.

"*Ach*, that is the best news ever!"

"*Jah*, maybe we can finally marry Judah off," Shiloh teased.

As the evening wore on and Mikey joined everyone for supper, Shiloh's anxiety slowly ebbed away. Mikey and *Dat* had pretty much dominated the conversation at the table, talking about work and customers coming to drop their lawnmowers for Mikey to work on, and all that guy stuff.

When he looked her way with a smile and a wink, she knew she had nothing to worry about. She would trust her beloved. After all, they'd both vowed to remain faithful and true to each other all their days. Peace filled her when she realized she had nothing to worry about.

TWENTY-TWO

Mikey glanced over at Shiloh across the breakfast table. *Ach*, he didn't get nearly as much time with his *fraa* as he wanted to. He'd began praying his small engine mechanic business would take off so he could stay home more.

And there had been something about Shiloh lately that he couldn't put his finger on. For some reason, she didn't seem as happy as when they'd first moved here and gotten hitched. But maybe it was natural for some of the enthusiasm to die down.

"My family would like us to come over for supper. How do you feel about tonight?" He munched on a slice of crisp bacon.

A smile lit up her face. "Tonight sounds *gut*."

He frowned. "*Dat* said he had something important he wanted to talk about. Do you think maybe he'll open up about his folks?"

"*Ach*, I don't know. We *have* been praying about it. And I know we've only had two fasting days so far, but do you think *Gott* is answering our prayers already?"

Excitement filled him. "It's possible."

"I didn't expect it to happen this soon."

"*Jah*, me neither." He squeezed her hand. "We'll have to keep praying."

"I think I'll skip lunch today and pray instead."

He grinned at her suggestion. "I'll do the same."

Several hours later, Shiloh helped *Mamm* with the supper dishes while *Grossdawdi* Sammy, *Dat*, and Mikey ushered the younger *kinner* outside to play.

Mikey leaned against the porch rail, allowing *Dat* and *Grossdawdi* to lounge on the porch swing. "You said you had something you wanted to talk about?" He eyed *Dat*.

Dat glanced at *Grossdawdi*. "We'll wait until *Mamm* comes out. I think it would be best if everyone was here."

A few moments later, *Mamm* and Shiloh and the oldest siblings all gathered around.

Dat began speaking. "This may or may not come as a shock to all of you, except for *Mamm* and *Dawdi*—they already know."

Mikey puzzled over what *Dat* could mean. *Mamm*

didn't know about *Dawdi* Walt and *Mammi* Edna, as far as Mikey knew.

Dat sighed. "You all have another sibling. A half sibling. An *Englisch* brother. His name is Maddox. Mikey, he's about a year younger than you are."

"What? How long have you known this?"

"I don't know. Since Maddox was about twelve, I guess."

Mikey rubbed his forehead and glanced at Shiloh. *Ach*, this wasn't what he'd been expecting at all.

"Anyway, I've got some pretty steep child support back payments. I can't afford to pay it right now, and jail time is out of the question, so I'm taking a job in Madison."

Jail time?

His mother gasped. Apparently, she hadn't known that part.

Dat looked at *Mamm*. "Sorry, Miri. It's just going to be the graveyard shift, so I'll still be home during the day to help with the *kinner*."

"You still need to sleep," *Mamm* insisted.

"*Jah*, I know." *Dat* looked at Mikey and each of his siblings. "I'm going to need all of you to help *Mamm* out more."

"How much money do you owe?" Mikey asked.

"You don't need to know that." *Dat's* frown deepened.

Mikey's lips tugged downward. This wasn't *gut*. *Dat* already had enough stress in his life. He glanced at *Grossdawdi* Sammy, who'd kept quiet this entire time. Apparently, he wasn't going to step in and stop *Dat*.

Shiloh studied Mikey on their way home. He'd been quiet since his *vatter's* revelation. Her heart went out to him. Surely, it couldn't be easy learning something like that. Apparently, his *vatter* had messed up his family tree pretty bad.

But maybe that wasn't a *gut* way to look at it. *Gott* was the one who determined life and death. Who was *she* to judge whether anyone's life was a burden? The Bible said *kinner* were a reward. It didn't mention how those *kinner* came into the world. *Der Herr* had a purpose and plan for each of them.

Thoroughly convicted, she hung her head. Who could know the mind of the Lord? She surely did not.

She reached for Mikey's hand. "Are you okay?"

"*Jah*, just thinking about things. And how blessed I am." He raised a sad smile. "That could have been me raised in the *Englisch* world. Almost was."

She had to laugh. "Yet you're choosing to live *Englisch* now."

"Only halfway." He winked. "Besides, I have an Amish heritage. I grew up around a strong community who supports one another and with a *gut* hard work ethic. Not perfect, mind you, but I am thankful for it."

"And you have a *gut* family."

"That's what I was thinking. It's just too bad *Dat* is on the outs with *Dawdi* and *Mammi*. You know they wouldn't hesitate to help him out if he asked."

She shook her head. "There is no way he would ask."

"*Jah*, I know." He stared at her. "But what if *I* did?"

TWENTY-THREE

Mikey examined the two lawnmowers, three ATVs, and motorcycle in the side yard next to the trailer. He chuckled to himself. *Ask, and ye shall receive.*

"Thank You, Lord." He whispered a brief prayer for *Gott's* provision.

Der Herr had blessed him with a *gut* amount of work. He might have to take time off from the feedstore to complete these projects in a timely manner for his customers. Fortunately, he'd been able to get off work early today.

Mikey's head shot up. He had been busy working on one of the lawnmowers, when he heard a vehicle pulling into their lane. Good, Shiloh was back earlier than expected. He needed to go wash up in the trailer. She'd need help bringing in the things she had planned to bring back from her folks' place. It was amazing how much he missed her even if she'd only been gone a few hours.

A knock sounded on the door before he was able to open it. Strange. Shiloh didn't usually knock. His mouth turned down as his eyes collided, not with his *fraa*, but an attractive young *Englisch* woman. He couldn't help but notice her attire—a midriff halter top and short cutoff jeans.

He swallowed. "May I...help you?" Perhaps this young woman was lost.

"Yeah, I...uh..." She glanced behind her, as though she was surveying the area around the trailer.

He'd always tried to keep the place tidy, but that wasn't easy nowadays given his customers' projects. "Did you need something worked on?"

Her eyebrow lifted, but her face showed confusion.

"I'm a small engine mechanic."

She nodded slowly. "And *you're* Michael Eicher?"

"Well, most folks that know me call me Mikey, but yeah. Did someone send you here?" Perhaps she had vehicle trouble.

"I don't...how old are you?"

He frowned. What on earth did this girl want with him? He was quite certain that he didn't want her around here when Shiloh returned. The last thing he wanted was for her to think he was entertaining strange women while she was away. "Why do you ask?"

"You look too young." Her forehead wrinkled.

"What do you mean? Too young for what?"

"For the Michael Eicher I'm looking for."

"Perhaps you're looking for my father? His name is Michael Eicher too." Although, he couldn't imagine why this girl would be seeking out his father.

"Is he, like, in his forties?"

"Yeah."

"*Your* father?" Her hands twisted and she peered up at him through thick lashes. "My name is Renee. I think you might be my brother."

Mikey's eyes flew wide and his mouth gaped. His heartbeat pulsed in his ears. "Your brother?"

Oh boy. Mikey grimaced.

This was the *last* thing his family needed. His father must've really gotten around in his younger days.

"Are you related to Maddox?" He recalled the half-brother he'd just learned about.

"Maddox?" Her lips twisted. "I've never heard that name."

"How old are you?"

"I'm twenty. How old are you?"

"Twenty-four." He rubbed the back of his neck. "I don't mean to be rude or anything, but how do you know my *dat* is your father?"

Fortunately, she didn't seem put out by the question. She nodded. "My mom figured he might deny that I'm his, so she encouraged me to take a DNA test. Let's just say I'm ninety-nine percent sure that the Michael Eicher, who lives in this area and is in his forties, is my father. Besides, my mom wasn't the promiscuous type. Your—*our* dad was the only one."

He sighed. Did he really have any reason to *not* believe her?

He felt silly standing out there in the hot sun having a conversation. "Would you like to come in for a minute and have something to drink?"

"Yes. Thank you. It's a little warm out here."

He glanced at the clock in the trailer then sighed in relief. Shiloh had said she probably wouldn't be back for another hour or so. He had a little time. But he needed to get this conversation over with as quickly as possible just in case Shiloh *did* return soon.

Mikey handed Renee a cup of iced sweet tea and sat across from her at the small table. "I don't mean to be blunt, but why are you looking for my father? Rather, *our* father *now*?"

"I decided I want to go to college, and I'm enrolling for classes in the fall. It's not cheap. My mom has no money, so she suggested I get a hold of my 'dead-beat father' and make him pay for it."

Mikey frowned. "My father isn't a dead beat."

"Maybe not. But *my* father is." She shrugged. "I mean, I've never even met him, so..."

"Does he even know about you?"

"My mom said she sent him a letter when I was young and she was struggling financially—which he never responded to. But she didn't want to get involved with the courts and have to face him again. I think I was the result of a one-night stand." She stared at the plastic cup, tapping its sides. "If he looked anything like you, I can see why she fell for him."

Mikey shrugged. "They say we look a lot alike."

"I hope you're not like him."

"My *dat* isn't like that anymore. As for me, I'm a one-woman man. Which reminds me, she'll be coming home soon. It would probably be best if you weren't here. Sorry, I don't mean to be rude or anything."

"So, can you give me his address then so I can contact him?"

He frowned. "My father isn't in any position to send anyone to college. He has a houseful of children and a son he's paying back child support for."

His heart ached for his folks. No doubt, this whole situation would put even more strain on their marriage. How would *Mamm* feel about yet another child *Dat* fathered with some woman he probably didn't even know? Would it be best if Mikey just asked Renee to stay a secret?

"What do you expect me to do, then?" She tapped her foot.

"Okay. Uh, let me think for a minute." He closed his eyes and prayed for wisdom. "If I could get you the money for college, would you stay away?"

"Stay away?" She frowned.

"Yeah. Like *not* go and see my father. He's already under a lot of stress. I'm worried about what this might do to him." And *Mamm*.

"So, you don't want me to meet my father at all?"

He rubbed his forehead. "I know it sounds bad. But you said you're looking for money for college, right? Would you have tried to contact him otherwise?"

She frowned. "I don't know. Maybe eventually."

"If you could just maybe wait a couple of years."

"To go to college?"

"No. To meet *Dat*." He thought about mentioning that he was Amish, but that might make it easier for her to find him.

"I guess I don't have to meet him right now. I

mean, like you said, I have gone all these years without knowing him. What's a couple more? But what about college?"

"I'll tell you what. Give me your address and phone number. I'm not sure if I can get the money or not, but I can try. If I do, I'll get a hold of you." He touched her hand, his gaze urgent. "But you have to *promise* not to try to get a hold of *Dat*."

She sighed but conceded with a nod. "Okay. I guess it's worth it for college." She laughed. "Why does this feel like I'm accepting a bribe?"

"I assure you that is not what this is. My family is already stretched thin. Honestly, if this gets out, it could be the straw that breaks the camel's back."

She pulled out her cell phone. "Give me your number too so I know it's you when you call."

"Okay. But you can't call or text this number. Not unless I call or text you first, okay?"

Renee frowned. "So, I guess we don't get to hang out or anything? I was thinking it might be cool to have a sibling or two, even if we're just half."

"I'm sorry. Truly, I am. Maybe in the future? This is just not a *gut* time for our family." *Ach*, he felt bad. Truly. This was his flesh and blood sister, and he was just sending her away. But what else could he do? "It was nice to meet you, Renee." He walked her to the door.

"Yeah, you too." Her sad smile and glassy eyes almost made him rethink sending her away.

Almost.

TWENTY-FOUR

S hiloh's heart plunged straight to her stomach like she'd been on one of those rollercoaster rides she and Sierra had gone on several years ago. She hadn't expected her husband to be holding a scantily clad young woman in his arms the moment her driver pulled up to their trailer.

"It looks like your boyfriend is...uh...has company." Shiloh's driver glanced at her, a cynical eyebrow hefted upward.

Shiloh's chin trembled as her gaze trailed the young woman hurrying to a vehicle parked in their driveway. What? Did she and Mikey think Shiloh hadn't seen them? Did they think the woman disappearing would make the situation not have happened?

When Mikey hurried out to the vehicle to help with her things, Shiloh refused to look him in the eye. As a matter of fact, he could bring *all* the bags into the trailer.

Shiloh scurried from the vehicle, thankful she'd already squared up with the driver. Instead of helping Mikey, she made a beeline for the trailer's tiny bathroom. She needed a *gut* cry right now.

She heard Mikey enter the trailer. It sounded as though he dropped the bags on the table.

"Shiloh?"

She refused to answer Mikey. Her heart hurt too much.

"Shiloh. Come on."

"*Nee.*" She shook her head forcefully, even though Mikey couldn't see her through the door. "I want you to take me back home."

Silence reigned a few moments.

A gentle knock on the door made her startle. "Shi."

"Go away." She sniffled.

"No. We need to talk."

"I don't have anything to say to you." Actually, that wasn't true. She wanted nothing more than to throw the book at him right now. Or at least *a* book. How dare he!

"It's not what it looks like."

She couldn't help the laugh devoid of mirth that escaped her lips. "Right. And neither was the passion pink lipstick."

"What are you talking about?" He huffed. "Seriously,

Shi. Come on out so we can talk about this."

"I don't want to see you right now." She tried to keep the wail out of her voice, but it proved difficult.

"Baby…" She heard him sigh. "Okay, I'll give you some time."

She waited until she heard the trailer door close before stepping out of the bathroom. She unrolled a mountain of toilet paper into her palm, took a few squares, dabbed her eyes, and blew her nose.

Shiloh hated that she was the jealous type, but she couldn't help it. She was head-over-heels in love with Mikey and the thought that he…he…*ach*, she couldn't even bring the words to the forefront of her mind. The image of him with that girl had been bad enough.

She took no time to gather the few belongings she had and stuff them in a bag, all the while thrusting away her stupid tears.

Why had she let Mikey talk her into marrying him? Why had he wanted to get married if he just had in mind to cheat on her? Did he think she would just sit idly by and let him make a mockery of their marriage? *Nee, Englisch* marriage or no, she was *not* going to stand for unfaithfulness. It may not mean anything to him, but to her their vows were just as iron-clad as if they'd married in the Amish church. *She* had taken her vows seriously.

Mikey apparently only wanted one thing. Why did men have to be so *dumm*? Well, not all men. She was sure and certain *Dat* would never do that to *Mamm*.

Ach, how she missed home.

Mikey had no idea what he was going to say to Shiloh. It was just as he feared—she believed the worst. And there was nothing he could say about it to convince her otherwise. He couldn't tell her who Renee was. Until he figured some things out, *nobody* could know.

Did *Dat* have any clue that he'd fathered an *Englisch dochder* too? If so, he'd been really *gut* at keeping secrets. And now, *he* had to keep a secret.

He hated not being able to tell Shiloh the truth. Just a few words and everything would make sense.

If only he could convince her to give him the benefit of the doubt. But if the roles had been reversed and *he* saw *her* near the door of the trailer with a handsome young man, he would likely assume the worst too. As a matter of fact, he'd probably chase the guy down and disregard his nonresistant roots altogether. There was no way he'd stand for another man putting the moves on his *fraa*.

Ach, this entire situation was perplexing. He had

no idea what to do, except that he needed to talk to *someone.*

    Grossdawdi Sammy.

TWENTY-FIVE

S hiloh stood the moment she heard Mikey coming up the trailer steps. She had to stand her ground and not let him sweet talk her into staying here.

"Shi, are you ready to talk now?"

"I just want to go home." She blew her nose again.

"This *is* our home, *fraa*." He reached for her hand, but she pulled back like her skin had been seared.

"Don't!" She detested the vulnerability in her voice.

"Don't what?"

"Don't try to sweet talk me into staying."

Mikey lifted his eyes to the sky and let out a long sigh. "Shiloh, I'm not cheating on you. I promise."

She shook her head.

"Trust me, Shi. Have I ever cheated on you before?"

"I don't know. Have you?" Her voice pitched high

again. She hated letting Mikey think he'd won. She didn't want to give him the upper hand.

"No. And I wouldn't." His gaze bore into her, but she looked away.

"Right."

"You have to believe me, *lieb*."

"I saw you two with my own eyes, Mikey! There is no logical explanation for you to have an *Englisch* woman in your arms."

"There is, actually." He swallowed.

"Then *who* was she?"

"I can't say." He looked away. A sure sign of guilt.

"You can't say." She rolled her eyes. "Do you think I'm a complete idiot, Mikey? I have eyes. I know what I saw."

"You know what you *think* you saw."

Oh, brother. "I'm not playing this game. I will not stay here another minute with a manipulator and a liar."

His countenance crumpled. "Is that who you think I am, Shi?"

Goodness, he was a *gut* actor. His wounded look almost made her question her assumption.

But seriously, what other explanation *could* there be? She'd dismissed the last time she thought something might be going on, but to do it twice would be foolish on her part.

She's gone from the house for a few hours, comes home to find her husband holding another woman in his arms, then the moment they get caught she flees.

Her chin began trembling again and tears leaked from her eyes. "Yes."

"Fine, then." He grabbed the keys from the counter. "If you can't even trust me...if that's what you think of your husband, then let's go."

The ride home had been completely silent. It had been the worst ten minutes of Shiloh's life. She refused to even glance his way.

"Shiloh." Mikey sighed. "Look, that girl is my sister."

Shiloh stared at her husband. Did he actually think she would believe that? "Whatever, Mikey!" She jumped out and slammed the car door, then ran to her folks' house.

When Mikey peeled out of the driveway, Shiloh knew their relationship was over.

She should have known how it would go, getting married among the *Englisch*. It had obviously meant nothing to Mikey. She'd thought he was serious when he pledged his love to her in front of the justice of the peace.

If only she'd listened to *Mamm* and *Dat* in the first place.

Tears fell so fast she couldn't stop them. If this was what a broken heart felt like, she wouldn't wish it on her worst enemy.

TWENTY-SIX

Mikey had been going back and forth about whether to share his newfound information with *Grossdawdi* Sammy or not. On one hand, he needed to be able to talk to *somebody*. On the other hand, all this stress wasn't exactly *gut* for *Grossdawdi* either.

Somehow, though, Mikey knew his *grossdawdi* could handle it. Something told him *Grossdawdi* had endured a lot during his eight-plus decades.

Mikey parked his car in front of *Grossdawdi's* barn. *Grossdawdi* met him the moment he stepped out.

Mikey frowned. "Is *Dat* here?"

"*Nee.* He went to see about that new job."

"*Gut.* I need to talk to you."

"Let's take a ride in my buggy. I'll go tell your *mamm* what's going on, so she doesn't think I went off and had a heart attack somewhere." He chuckled.

"That's not funny, *Grossdawdi*." Mikey's heart tightened in his chest.

"Between you and me, *sohn*, I'm more worried about something like that happening with your *vatter* than myself."

Jah, that was Mikey's fear too. "That's why I came to talk to you."

A few minutes later, the two of them clip-clopped down the quiet country road.

Grossdawdi inhaled deeply. "Isn't this the best? Fresh spring air. Warm breezes. It's hard to have a care when you know *Gott* is so *gut*. Ain't so?"

"*Jah*." Mikey couldn't help his weighted sigh.

"What was that for?"

"Shiloh and I had a fight. She moved back in with her folks."

"Fights are normal, even when folks are in love." *Grossdawdi* asserted.

"I know. But how do you continue in a relationship if one person doesn't trust the other when they're telling the truth?"

"She doesn't trust you or you don't trust her?"

"She doesn't trust me."

"Why?"

"She thinks I'm cheating on her." He grimaced.

Grossdawdi's surprised expression widened. "And

why would she think that?"

"Because she saw me hugging a woman."

"I see."

"And that's what I wanted to talk to you about. I know you will keep a secret if I ask you to."

"So, you *are* cheating on her?" *Grossdawdi's* forehead wrinkled.

"*Nee*. Of course not. I would never."

"Never is a long time and none of us knows exactly how our future will go. I'm sure there are many who have said never and have fallen into a snare of the devil. We must take heed lest we fall." *Grossdawdi* warned.

"*Jah*, okay. But you know what I mean."

"Why were you hugging this woman?"

He glanced away as a vehicle passed them. "I think I need to start from the beginning."

"Go for it."

Mikey proceeded to tell *Grossdawdi* Sammy about the entire ordeal.

"I see." *Grossdawdi* sighed.

"Did I do the right thing by sending her away? *Dat* already has all this stress. I don't know how much more he can handle."

"You have a *gut* heart, *sohn,* to care for your family in this way." *Grossdawdi* covered Mikey's hand with his. "But this is not your burden to bear. Your father is reaping what he's sown."

"I know. But is it wrong to want to help?"

"*Nee*, it's not wrong."

"Do you have any advice for me?"

"*Jah*, pray. And then take your hands off the reins before your buggy crashes too."

"What does that mean?" He frowned.

"Go to your *aldi* and calmly explain everything to her. That is the first step." *Grossdawdi* advised.

"What about *Mamm* and *Dat*?"

"Let me handle your father, then he can share with your mother as he sees fit."

"*Grossdawdi*, are you still praying and fasting for the situation with *Mammi* and *Dawdi*?"

Grossdawdi nodded.

"*Gut*. I am too."

Now that Mikey had a plan in mind, it was time to set it into motion. When he left his folks' place, he would drive straight to the Millers' house and have a heart-to-heart with his *fraa*. And hopefully, he'd bring her back home.

TWENTY-SEVEN

Michael stared down at the large manilla envelope as he walked to the house in disbelief. He opened it up again and attempted to count the bills inside. He examined the typed note for any clue who it might be from.

He read the words, "Consider this a gift from God."

He turned the envelope over again. It had been postmarked locally. Where had this money come from? *Who* had this kind of money? No one around here that he could think of.

But there *was* someone who had plenty. This amount would only be a drop in the bucket for them. They would never send him money, though, because they knew he'd refuse it. Was that why this arrived anonymously?

Someone had to have contacted them about his

current financial situation. That was the only way this money could have arrived. And there were only a handful of people who knew.

He thought about Mikey's odd question a few weeks ago about his folks. Where had that come from? Moreover, how did he know anything about his folks or the situation?

Michael's head lifted as *Dawdi* Sammy's buggy made its way into the side yard and up to the barn. Mikey jumped down and began unhitching the horse from the buggy.

Michael tucked the envelope under his arm and strode toward them.

Dawdi eyed the envelope. "Whatcha got there?"

Mikey continued to remove the horse's harness. Was his *sohn* avoiding looking at him?

"It's an envelope full of money."

"You're kidding." *Dawdi* appeared to know nothing about it, which could only mean one thing. "Who's it from?"

"It says it's a gift from *Gott*. There was no return address and no sender name. I'm guessing the person or people who sent it want to remain anonymous."

"Interesting. How much is in there?"

"A lot. Enough to cover the back child support payments. And more."

Dawdi whistled low. "Does sound like a gift from *Der Herr*."

"*Jah*, but I can't accept it."

Mikey remained conspicuously silent and his shoulders sagged. A tell-tale sign he knew *exactly* what was going on.

Dawdi frowned now. "Why not?"

"Because it isn't from *Der Herr*. It's from the devil." His blood boiled just thinking about it.

"Now why would you go and say a thing like that?"

"Why don't you ask Mikey? He knows who it's from." Michael stared at his *sohn*. "Don't you?"

Mikey kept quiet still.

"Tell them I don't want their blood money." Michael shoved the envelope into his *sohn's* bosom. "And next time, don't go sticking your nose where it doesn't belong."

Michael turned and stomped back toward the house.

Mikey fisted away the tears that threatened. *Ach*, he'd only tried to help. *Dat* hadn't just become bitter over the years; he'd become hateful.

"You're a fool!" *Grossdawdi* Sammy hollered in *Dat's* direction.

Mikey's head snapped toward *Grossdawdi*. *Ach*,

the man was bold as a lion.

His *vatter* spun around and frowned at *Grossdawdi*. "What?"

"You heard me. But in case you didn't, let me say it again. You're a fool *and* a coward."

"How is that?" *Dat* scowled.

"This *bu* has more courage and family loyalty than you could ever dream of having. Not only that, but he has a heart of gold."

"He's working with the devil." *Dat* challenged.

"*Nee. You* are the only one working for the devil. Mikey has only tried to bring peace and reconciliation to this family. *Blessed are the peacemakers, for they shall be called the children of God.*" *Grossdawdi* took the envelope from Mikey. "This money did not come from your folks. It came from your *sohn*. It was his inheritance. It was his future with his *fraa*. The one he gave up in order to protect his ungrateful *vatter*."

Ach. How did *Grossdawdi* know that? Had he spoken with *Dawdi* or *Mammi* Eicher?

"What are you talking about?" *Dat* glanced at *Grossdawdi*, then at Mikey.

"Why don't you actually talk to your *sohn* instead of accusing him of something he hasn't even done?" And with that, *Grossdawdi* Sammy walked away, leaving the two of them alone in the middle of the yard.

Ach, how had he ever doubted *Grossdawdi* Sammy? He certainly deserved a fierce hug.

Dat now stared at him. "What was he talking about?"

"Which part?" Mikey frowned.

"The part about you giving up your life with Shiloh to protect me."

"I wasn't going to tell you about it." He shifted from one foot to the other.

"Tell me about what?"

His expression sobered and he stared at his *vatter.* "Your *Englisch dochder.*"

"My *what*? I don't have an *Englisch dochder.*"

"Apparently you do. And she expects you to pay for her college."

"*What*?" *Dat* removed his hat and his hand plowed through his hair.

"Her name is Renee. She's twenty years old. She came and saw me the other day. She was looking for you. You were already stressed out about the whole back child support thing. I told her not to contact you and that I'd figure out a way to get her money for college. I didn't ask her mother's name. Renee said she thought she was conceived in a one-night stand, so you probably wouldn't remember anyway."

"She said all that?" *Dat* pinched the bridge of his

nose. "And what about Shiloh?"

"She saw me with Renee and assumed the worst. I tried to tell Shiloh that Renee was my half-sister, but she didn't believe me. She thought I was cheating on her and moved out of the trailer and back to her folks' place." *Ach*, the fact still wrenched his heart.

"And what about the money?" *Dat* clenched the envelope.

"What about it?"

"*Who* is it from?"

"Me. So much for trying to do a good deed and remain anonymous." Mikey rolled his eyes.

"It's not from your *Mammi* and *Dawdi* Eicher?"

"*Jah*. It's my inheritance from them to do with as I pleased. They mentioned nothing about you."

"I don't want to take your inheritance." *Dat* attempted to hand the envelope back, but Mikey refused.

"There's plenty more. Believe me." Mikey smiled. "Please use it so you can stay home and help *Mamm*. She deserves it." Tears burned in his eyes.

"You're right. She does." *Dat* put a hand on his shoulder and squeezed, his eyes misting over. "*Denki.* This means a lot. You are a *gut sohn.*"

"It's my pleasure."

"And forgive me for judging you harshly. I should

be the one who is an example to you. I have failed you in this area. And probably many others."

Mikey nodded.

"About the college thing. You're not paying that out of your inheritance too, are you?"

"*Nee. Dawdi* Walt said, *A righteous man leaveth an inheritance for his children's children.* And that's what he aims to do. No matter how many of us there are." Mikey chuckled.

"Is that what he said?"

Mikey laughed. "Why don't you call him and find out? It's long overdue."

Dat took a hard breath. "I'll think about it."

TWENTY-EIGHT

Michael drew Miri to his side as they strode up to the entrance of his folks' place. Seeing the house and property brought back bittersweet memories, although he'd held onto the bitter so fiercely that he hardly remembered the sweet ever existed.

It seemed like everything came rushing back at once. The pain and sorrow he'd felt over losing Jessica. The rage he'd felt toward his folks. When he'd shaken the dust off his boots and left all those years ago, he couldn't even see straight. And then he'd gone on to make a complete mess of his life, damaging who knows how many others in the process.

He'd sworn he would never return. Yet, here he was.

Somehow, Mikey's tenderheartedness had crept into Michael's own soul. He couldn't help the pride in his heart, knowing what a great person his *sohn* had turned out to be. After all the ways his *dumm vatter* had fumbled things up, Mikey remained an inspiration.

Michael took a deep breath before he knocked on the door. He knew this conversation was long overdue.

As soon as the door opened, his heart filled with overwhelming emotion.

Mamm and *Dat* stood there, obvious signs of age lined their faces. *Dat's* jaw trembled. "*Sohn*, you've finally come home."

Unable to stop himself, he lunged into his *Dat's* arms. Sobbing wracked his body as all the years of brokenness melted away. He'd needed this release for far too long.

When he was finally able to speak, he pulled his *fraa* near. "*Jah*, I've come home. Please meet my *fraa*, Miriam."

Shiloh swallowed hard as she knocked on the trailer door.

She hadn't seen Mikey in days. Not since he'd dropped her off in her folks' driveway and squealed out onto the road like his car was on fire. She supposed she deserved that.

It wasn't until she received a visit from Mikey's *dat*

yesterday that she realized her mistake. He'd also informed her of what Mikey had done for their family, and apologized for his own shortcomings. It had been a *gut* visit indeed.

Now that she knew the truth about Mikey, she needed to confess her transgression.

As soon as the door opened, the floodgates opened with it. Mikey stood there looking so forlorn and she could barely stand to see him in such a state.

She rushed up the metal steps, slammed the door behind herself, and plowed into him, giving him no choice but to wrap his arms around her.

"I'm sorry!" Her words came out on a sob. "Sorry for accusing you of something you didn't do."

"*Jah*, me too." He stared down into her eyes and captured her lips with his. "I'm just glad to have my *fraa* back."

"Please, forgive me?" She searched his eyes.

"I don't blame you, Shi. I don't know if I wouldn't have done the same thing if the tables had been reversed. But I hope I would at least give you the benefit of the doubt."

"I know. But after the lipstick on your clothes and then—"

"What lipstick are you talking about?"

"The pink mark on the collar of your work shirt."

"*Ach*, why didn't you say anything about that? I would have told you about the pesky *Englisch* woman who comes into the feedstore. She always tries to get her hands on me. That time, she was removing something from my collar, she'd said."

Shiloh's eyes widened. "With her mouth?"

"*Nee.* Her fingers. But they had been touching her bright pink lips before that. I had planned to tell you then forgot all about it." He chuckled. "Shows how much it meant to me. That woman is a nuisance."

"Well, seeing that girl in your arms, which I now know was your sister, I freaked out and I ran. In my mind, there was no logical explanation for what I saw except that you'd been cheating on me. And then, with you working all those hours...I was devastated. I thought I'd lost you."

"You didn't lose me, *lieb*." He sighed, drew her into his arms, and held her close. "You'll never lose me."

"I'm sorry."

"I just wish you trusted me more." He frowned. "A *gut* marriage has to be built on trust. I love you and there is no other woman who will ever come close to comparing to you."

Tears burned in her eyes. "I love you too."

"Let's go talk to our folks tonight about our plans to marry, *jah*?"

She nibbled on her lip. "About that. I kind of already spilled the beans to our folks that we were married among the *Englisch*."

"You what?" His jaw dropped. "But I thought you wanted an Amish wedding?"

"Oh, I still do. *Dat* talked to Jerry Bontrager and he already okayed it." Trying to contain her smile was like trying to hide the sun. "Until then, we will live here as husband and wife."

"*Gut.* Because we now own this land. I bought it with my inheritance from *Dawdi* and *Mammi* Eicher."

Joy bubbled up inside her. "*Ach*, for real?"

"Only a hundred acres of it, but *jah*. This trailer, the meadow, the woods, the pond. It's all ours now." He grinned. "And we can build a real house whenever we want."

"Have I ever told you how much I love you?"

"You can say it a million times and I'll never tire of it." Her husband leaned down and claimed her lips once again.

EPILOGUE

*T*heir wedding day had been *wunderbaar*, but the celebration continued. Shiloh and Mikey had encouraged their family and friends to join them at their property for a weekend of camping.

Even *Mammi* and *Dawdi* Eicher had come all the way from Pennsylvania and rented a special RV for the occasion. Now, everyone had gathered around the campfire roasting marshmallows and singing and telling stories that she would likely remember for as long as she lived.

Her father-in-law had made amends with his folks at long last. And even though they'd invited Mikey's newfound *Englisch* half-siblings to their wedding, they hadn't shown up.

Michael and Mikey had joined forces and decided to build a mechanic shop on the edge of their property out near the road. So far, they had enough work to keep them busy into the foreseeable future. Shiloh was quite certain *Gott* would be providing more.

As far as camping went, they'd invited *Grossdawdi* Sammy to stay in the trailer with them. They'd laughed when he'd said, "You must think I'm *ferhoodled* if you expect me to share a trailer with newlyweds."

Instead, he'd opted for one of the extra beds in *Mammi* Edna and *Dawdi* Walt's rented RV. Shiloh and Mikey had guessed that a reunion between them had been long overdue.

Shiloh knew she had to be the most blessed woman that ever lived in the history of time. And she was sure and certain of that fact because of all the miracles she'd seen in her life and the lives of those around her.

Their lives were living proof that all things are possible with *Gott*, the Healer.

THE END

Look for *The Newcomer* (Amish Country Brides) coming in August 2022, Lord willing!
The Newcomer is the Prequel to the series – how it all began!

It's not too late to subscribe to my newsletter! Get a FREE Amish story as my thank you gift when you sign up for my newsletter here: www.jenniferspredemann.com

Have you read Justin and Lucy's story?

The Arrangement (Amish Spring Romance)

A handsome Amish bachelor. A bishop's daughter in trouble. An unexpected marriage.

When Bishop Bontrager's teen daughter, Lucy, becomes pregnant with an *Englischer's* baby, he's determined to keep her in their Amish community—and find a *gut* Amish husband for her.

Amish bachelor Justin Beachy is shocked when the bishop approaches him with an outlandish plan to marry his young daughter—and keep her pregnancy a secret. But, as crazy as the bishop's plan seems, Justin's compassionate heart won't allow him to decline the proposal.

Lucy reluctantly agrees to a marriage of convenience, but will her agreement end in resentment toward her new husband, her father, and the Amish church?

Can Justin and Lucy discover God's blessings in their lives and navigate their way to happily-ever-after?

Available in ebook, paperback, and hardcover.
Get your copy here:

https://books2read.com/u/bx1ggJ

Dear Reader,

I hope you enjoyed Shiloh and Mikey's story. I can hardly believe they're all grown up!

Did you like learning more about the Eicher family history? That Michael... But even with all his past mistakes and failures, God still showed him mercy and gave him another chance.

Aren't you glad God sees through completely different eyes than how others see us or how we see ourselves? He deeply loves us and proved it when He sent Jesus to die on the cross for our sins. What great and terrible and wonderful love! And the great thing about His love is that it is eternal. Forever. Everlasting. No matter how bad we try to mess up our lives, He promises to never leave us or forsake us.

Isn't that a *wunderbaar gut* promise? I think it's the best news ever!

The main theme of this book is healing. God is the ultimate healer. Is there an area in your life that needs healing today? Go to the Healer. Cast your cares upon Him and see if He doesn't take your pain and replace it with something magnificent.

To GOD be the glory!

Thanks for reading.

Blessings in Christ,
Jennifer Spredemann
Heart-Touching Amish Fiction

P.S. Word of mouth is one of the best forms of advertisement and a HUGE blessing to the author. If you enjoyed this book, **please** consider leaving a review, sharing on social media, and telling your reading friends.

DISCUSSION QUESTIONS

1. At the onset, Shiloh is planning to defy her parents. Growing up, did you ever do anything that went directly against your parents' wishes?

2. Although Shiloh was raised in a good, God-fearing home, she still makes her own choices. Do you have children who have made poor choices that pain you?

3. In the beginning, Mikey is angry with Sammy because he felt like he'd been unjustly punished (and perhaps betrayed by his *grossdawdi*.) Have you ever felt that way toward a loved one?

4. Because of his own past (which readers are going to find out about soon!) Sammy thinks time in jail will encourage Mikey to walk the straight and narrow. Do you agree with Sammy's decision? Why or why not?

5. Mikey and Shiloh decide to keep their marriage a secret. Did you expect Shiloh to end up in the *familye* way and having to explain to everyone?

6. Mikey meets his paternal grandparents at twenty-four. Are there any close relatives in your life now that you hadn't known growing up?

7. When Mikey enters the scene for the first time, he seems to be rebellious—or at least make unwise decisions. We don't trust him at first, mostly because of others' perceptions of him. What were you expecting from Mikey's character?

8. Michael Eicher has held onto bitterness for a long time. Have you ever carried something on your shoulders that would have been better carried by the Lord?

9. Like Mikey, most people have great love and respect for their mother. Tell us about yours.

10. From the very beginning, I feel that Mikey is harshly judged by others based on his father's mistakes. Have you ever been judged because of the behavior of a family member or friend?

11. Have you ever judged someone else based on one of their relatives? (I feel sorry for the families of criminals who are probably often judged by their loved one's poor actions.)

12. Who was your favorite character in the story and why? (For me, I loved Mikey's character. He surprised me at many turns. Who knew he had a heart of gold?)

A SPECIAL THANK YOU

I would like to express a *special* thank you to all my readers, who helped with the names in this book. To readers, **Tammy Layton** and **Kris Kauffman Houck**, thank you for suggesting the names "Walter" and "Edna" for Mikey's grandparents.

I'd like to take this time to thank everyone that had any involvement in this book and its production, including my Mom and Dad, who have always been supportive of my writing, my longsuffering Family— especially my handsome, encouraging Hubby, my Amish and former-Amish friends who have helped immensely in my understanding of the Amish ways, my supportive Pastor and Church family, my Proofreaders, my Editor, my Author friends, my wonderful Readers who buy, read, offer great input, and leave encouraging reviews and emails, my awesome Launch Team who, I'm confident, will 'Sprede the Word' about *The Healer*! And last, but certainly not least, I'd like to thank my ***Precious LORD and SAVIOUR JESUS CHRIST***, for without Him, none of this would have been possible!

If you haven't joined my Facebook reader group,
you may do so here:
https://www.facebook.com/groups/379193966104149/

Made in United States
Troutdale, OR
09/28/2024

23190388R00116